MW00806175

The Twelve Dancing Princesses
AND OTHER FAIRY TALES

The Twelve Dancing Princesses

AND OTHER FAIRY TALES

Retold by Sir Arthur Quiller-Couch

Illustrated by Kay Nielsen

PORTLAND HOUSE
New York

This collection of fairy tales was originally entitled
In Powder and Crinoline.

This 1988 edition is published by Portland House, a division of dilithium Press, Ltd., distributed by
Crown Publishers, Inc.,
225 Park Avenue South, New York, New York 10003.

Printed and Bound in the United States of America

Library of Congress Cataloging-in-Publication Data

Quiller-Couch, Arthur Thomas, Sir, 1863–1944.
The twelve dancing princesses / retold by Sir Arthur Quiller-Couch ; illustrated by Kay Nielsen.
Contents: Minon-Minette—Felicia, or, The pot of pinks—The twelve dancing princesses—Rosanie, or, The inconstant prince—The man who never laughed—John and the ghosts—The czarina's violet.
ISBN 0-517-67584-6
1. Fairy tales. [1. Fairy tales. 2. Folklore.] I. Nielsen, Kay Rasmus, 1886–1957, ill. II. Title. III. Title: 12 dancing princesses.
PZ8.Q42Tw 1988
398.2′1—dc19 88-22933
CIP
AC

h g f e d c b a

CONTENTS

COLOR ILLUSTRATIONS

Illustrations

Illustrations

FOREWORD

As you page through the stories in *The Twelve Dancing Princesses and Other Fairy Tales*, you will find yourself in shadowy, dreamlike lands whose unfamiliar terrains and strange inhabitants can suddenly disclose similarities with our everyday world. Writing in the first quarter of this century, Sir Arthur Quiller-Couch bequeathed to us elegantly written and often witty stories that continue to speak to the modern reader. Quiller-Couch's collaborator, the Danish artist Kay Nielsen, provided 24 color plates for this collection ranging from the romantic and ethereal to the menacing and bizarre. Nielsen's highly stylized figures and ornate designs complement Quiller-Couch's breezy narrative, while the bold lines and eerie palette used in the more disquieting illustrations emphasize the darker aspects of these tales.

Mirroring the real world, fairy tale lands contain both good and evil, the logical and the nonsensical, reward and punishment. A relationship with the real is helpful to the young child who is always looking to extend the field of his knowledge and, in some sense, to gain mastery of his environment. The fairy tale, then, can point children in new directions of thought and help to confirm already established beliefs about the way in which the world operates. It is important for young readers to see fairyland wrong-doers suitably punished, the kindhearted rewarded with the love of a prince or a princess, and the frivolous taught the merits of hard work. Children need to test the validity of such values—they need to know whether industriousness, honesty, and generosity truly are prized by society as their parents and teachers tell them. By affirming the standards children have been taught to respect, fairy tales bring a reassuring sense of order to an often confusing, chaotic world.

Quiller-Couch's delightfully entertaining stories make use of the ability to instruct or to comment upon a child's development. In *Minon-Minette*, for example, the young Prince Souci must learn to reason and master the conventional codes of acceptable social behavior. When we meet him, he is virtually a blank slate:

> . . . he lacked the first secret of pleasing, which is the desire to please; and he who lacks this can never possess attractive manners. In short, he was a good-looking fellow, who had never been taught to know the world or to use his brains.

Clearly, young Souci needs tutelage and it is the Fairy Aveline who decides to take on this task. Through her magic, Souci is deprived of his squire, horse, and sword, and is sent off into the world on a series of adventures that teach him humility, responsibility, and sound reasoning. While a prisoner of the evil Iron King, Souci exclaims, "Kings ought to set a good example, which you are very far from doing . . ." and we observe the signs of his development into a paragon of princes. At the end of his training, we are well-satisfied with his reward—his betrothal to his tutor's beautiful ward, Minon-Minette.

Prince Souci is but one of many characters found in this charming collection from whom children can learn. The heroine of *Felicia*, a Cinderella-like girl who does not allow the wickedness of her brother or the meanness of her circumstances to poison her good nature, finds herself magically transformed by a fairy she has befriended. She "...saw her poor cotton frock changed to a robe of silver brocade embroidered with carbuncles [jewels]," and over her head appeared "...a veil of gauze and gold, crowned with a coronet of diamonds." In *The Man Who Never Laughed*, we watch with horror as a comely young man's features wither and age as a punishment for his overpowering avarice. The transformation of his face mirrors the degeneration of his soul.

As well as reinforcing good conduct, this collection of tales evokes familiar emotions experienced in childhood. In *The Twelve Dancing Princesses*, we find twelve sisters who, in essence, do not yet wish to leave the nursery. When the youngest alone realizes that someone has followed them to their hidden underground world and discovered the secret of their worn shoes, she trembles not only with fear at the thought of growing up, but also with the realization and acceptance of the inevitability of change.

These enchanting stories and Quiller-Couch's waggish presentation of them are but half of this volume's allure. Kay Nielsen's fully realized illustrations distill the essence of these characters and their lives in a way that makes us catch our breaths as we turn to them. Whether it be the pale, minimalist drawing of a forlorn princess who had not smiled once in a whole year, or the stern aspect of the Iron King in his black throne room, or a comic peek at a dandyish prince who has taken to his bed after not getting his way, these portraits linger in the mind's eye.

Foreword

Given the quality of his work as seen here, it is difficult to understand Nielsen's failure to retain his hold on the acclaim accorded him in his early years as an artist. After the success of the illustrations for both this volume and for a collection of folk tales entitled *East of the Sun and West of the Moon*, Nielsen conquered the theatrical arena as chief stage designer for the Danish State Theater. In the 1930s he ventured to Hollywood, hoping to make his mark in the film industry, but work as a set designer was offered only infrequently and soon not at all. In order to eke out a living, he subsequently labored as a chicken farmer, and during the ensuing years he was rarely called on to use his skills as an artist. One of his few projects—a mural for a Los Angeles high school—was unceremoniously demolished only one year after its completion due to building renovations. Nielsen died in 1957, his unique and intriguing vision of fairyland long since forgotten. Now, with this edition of *The Twelve Dancing Princesses and Other Fairy Tales*, his magic again can be enjoyed by new generations of parents and children, which seems a fitting tribute to an artist who took for his subject worlds of the imagination—lands of boundless possibility.

LEE SANTINI
Editor

New York
1988

EDITORIAL NOTE

The modern reader may be surprised to discover old-fashioned expressions, styles of punctuation, and spelling, but these have been retained to convey the flavor of the original work.

PREFACE

THE genius of the young artist who has illustrated this book may be left to speak for itself, as it assuredly will: but I would say a word about the title, which is also of his invention.*

When the publishers told me that Mr. Kay Nielsen wished to employ both his pencil and his fanciful imagination upon a volume of Fairy Tales, to be called *In Powder and Crinoline*, I answered that the title and the notion it

*This collection of fairy tales was originally entitled *In Powder and Crinoline.*

conveyed were, in my opinion, capital; that no-one with forty-one volumes of the *Cabinet des Fées* on his shelves (to name that collection alone) ought to find any difficulty with *Powder* save the pleasant difficulty of choosing; but that if anyone knew where to find in the age of *Crinoline* a stock of such tales as we wanted I should be obliged by the information. There was no doubt they *ought* to exist, but I doubted very much if they did.

So, or nearly so, it turned out. The first four stories in this volume are drawn from an almost inexhaustible treasury. *Minon-Minette* comes from a *Bibliothèque des Fées et des Génies* collected by the Abbé de la Porte (who found this particular tale in a previous collection, *Le Pot-Pourri: Ouvrage de ces Dames et de ces Messieurs*. It has been attributed to the Comte de Caylus). *Felicia* is rendered from the *Fortunée* of the Comtesse d'Aulnoy: *Rosanie* from de Caylus *(Féeries Nouvelles)*: while for *The Twelve Dancing Princesses* I went to Mr. Andrew Lang—to whom the children of this generation owe a public monument—and obtained leave to adapt the version in his *Red Fairy Book*. In one of his last letters he granted me this, the last of many friendly favours.

But for *Crinoline*, after an unavailing search, I had to use expedients. It seems absurd—it *is* absurd—that few fairy tales or none should have been bequeathed to us by our grandmothers who wore crinolines and practised Cupid's own sport of archery, or by our grandfathers who wore peg-top trousers and Dundreary whiskers, and built the Crystal Palace and drove to the Derby in green-veiled top hats having Dutch dolls stuck about the brim. The mischief with them appears to have lain in the generation preceding: they were the very soil for fairy tales, but, in an evangelical age, they had been taught none in the nursery, and so they had no material of young romance to play upon and sophisticate as *Ces Dames et ces Messieurs*—de Caylus, Madame d'Aulnoy and the rest—so prettily played upon and sophisticated the themes that Charles Perrault recollected from the gossip of his old nurse.

It was a thousand pities: and I yet cherish a hope that someone will come forward, before it is too late, to people the Great Exhibition of 1851 with fairies and set them dancing around the crinolines and tall hats of that period. The purveyor of the following 'letter-press' has indicated rather than supplied that urgent need in our literature. The story of *The Man Who Never Laughed* is adapted from an Eastern tale of which Morris made use in *The Earthly Paradise*, and (if I may say it, in all respect to that great man) not the best use. The original has a polite cynicism which—lost in Morris's romantic and somewhat wordy treatment—seemed to me worth an effort to preserve. For *John and the Ghosts* I fell back on a short story of my own. To speak strictly, it is not all my own, but was composed with the help of a friend in the course of an idle day's yachting. Lastly, for *The Czarina's Violet* I had recourse to an anecdote of Prince Bismarck quoted in *The Poet's Charter* by my friend Mr. Francis Money-Coutts, now Lord Latimer.

This confession tells, all too plainly, that I have taken my good things (if good they be) where I happened to find them: but the following pages may suggest to some young writer of Genius that there is not only a crying need for Fairy Tales of the *Crinoline* period but an Artist waiting for him to rise up and supply it.

Arthur Quiller-Couch.

The Twelve Dancing Princesses
AND OTHER FAIRY TALES

MINON-MINETTE

IN the days when the *Fairies* were in request at every royal christening, there lived a young king whose name was *Souci*. His parents had died when he was quite young, and he had been brought up from boyhood by his godmother, the *Fairy Girouette*.

This *Girouette* was a thoroughly well-meaning fairy: but she suffered from the defect of never knowing her own mind for ten minutes together. As her will veered about like a weathercock, so the affairs of the country— over which she held absolute sway during the prince's minority—were all at sixes and sevens. To make matters worse, after training him up to obey her every caprice and (albeit with no ill intent) doing her worst to quench in him all sense of responsibility with every spark of "initiative"—as it is called—of a sudden she found that pressing business called her away to a neighbouring kingdom; whereupon off she went, having resigned to young *Souci* the reins of government which he was all unskilled to handle.

One wise thing she did in her flighty haste to depart. She summoned a Council of the Realm and named as *Prime Minister* the very worthy *Ditto*—so called because he had never been known to contradict anybody. This habit of complaisance had recommended him to the *Fairy* in times past as a statesman to be trusted. "You can," she would say, "rely on *Ditto* to agree when all else fails."

Young *Prince Souci* had a personable face and figure, and also—when you reached it—a fund of common-sense. But he lacked the first secret of pleasing, which is the desire to please; and he who lacks this can never possess attractive manners. In short, he was a good-looking fellow, who had never been taught to know the world or to use his brains. *Girouette* had happened to say once, "I wish *Souci* to grow up shy: nothing is more charming in a Prince":—and, strange to say, she had never afterwards said the exact opposite, possibly because she had never given the remark a second thought. But *Souci's* governesses and tutors had remembered the hint and so far improved on it that when he came to govern the smallest event took him by surprise. "Dear me!" he would exclaim when any new affair of state came up to be discussed. And his counsellors, whether because they suffered an equal astonishment or (it is possible) to flatter him, would echo "Dear me!" while one or two, just to show that they were independent and thought for themselves, would add "Well, I never!"

The policy of this Council, helped by the *King's* total neglect of all details of business, led to some disorder in the finances of the realm, and finally to an open rebellion, in the midst of which it must be confessed that *Souci* exhibited remarkable presence of mind. When an armed mob threatened the palace, he sent for his flageolet and, upon a second thought, for his *Prime Minister*. "You sing while I play," commanded *Souci*, and the *Prime Minister* obeyed readily: for, to begin with, it was his duty—secondly, he never could say no to anyone, least of all to his sovereign—thirdly, he had a neat baritone voice, and had never in his life found so large an audience for it—and lastly, the words and air were extremely appropriate to the situation. The song ran:

When everything is said,
 There's nothing left to say:
So we'll all go to bed,
 Ri-tooral-looral-lay!

One can never predict what will inflame or, on the contrary, tranquillise the passions of the lower orders. The rebels, impressed by their monarch's gay unconcern, set it down to confidence in a reserve of force of which they knew nothing: and dispersed, not without mutual accusations of treachery. The popular upheaval died down as quickly as it had arisen, without effusion of blood, and the news-sheets next day were loud in their praises of the young king for what they called his "handling of the crisis."

The rebellion had no sooner died down, however, than *Ditto* proposed to the Council that the *King* really ought to marry. In the event of further trouble it would be indispensible to have a female voice to take the high notes. "My own register," said *Ditto* modestly, "is not what it was: and moreover"—here he glanced down on his ample waist—"a queen, if she be young and beautiful and of the right lineage, must necessarily produce an impression with which I cannot hope to vie. We did pretty well the other day," continued *Ditto*, yet more modestly. "But we have to think of next time. Fore-warned is fore-armed."

The Council applauded his wisdom and chose a Committee of Selection. The Committee met, and after considering the names of several eligible neighbouring Princesses, found themselves unable to decide. In their perplexity they resolved to send a letter to the *Fairy Girouette*, respectfully demanding her advice.

The *Fairy Girouette* answered by return of post that she would not presume to dictate to the *King* and his Council, but that, for her part, she suggested the *Princess Diaphanie*, only child of a monarch whose kingdom lay to the south-west, as the most suitable bride for *Prince Souci*.

Prime Minister Ditto said ditto, of course; and accordingly envoys were sent to bring back report concerning the *Princess Diaphanie*, her looks and behaviour, and whether she would make a good wife for *Prince Souci*, who in the meanwhile practised a new tune on his flageolet.

The envoys returned and reported that the *Princess Diaphanie* was fair and well made; that she was commendable, indeed, at every point save one. She was so light and ethereal that the grooms who rode with her, and the ladies who walked with her, had always to be on the watch lest the wind should carry her off. The court poets sang of her that she could tread the meadows without crushing a flower and pass over the waters without wetting her feet or dimpling a wave. These flatteries were all very well, so far as they went, and held truth enough to pass muster. But for practical purposes and lest they should lose her, her parents had to weight her pockets and the soles of her shoes; to keep her indoors whenever there was a wind; while, to make matters sure, she was never allowed abroad without six attendants, each of whom held one end of a string, of which the other was fastened to her waist.

The report of the envoys was put into writing and submitted, before presentation to Council, to the *Grand*

Hair-splitter, an official invented by the *Fairy Girouette*, who had straightway forgotten his existence. The *Grand Hair-splitter*, indeed, was practising upon his own wig for lack of anything better to do, when he received this unexpected commission. At once he flung himself with his whole heart upon the task: and within ten days he had separated the envoy's report into no less than five hundred *pros* and *cons* (with an appendix and schedules of 'doubtful cases' or 'cases reserved'). He presented the result of his labour to the Council, with an introductory statement in which he did not hesitate to declare his opinion that, taking one thing with another, there was a deal to be said more or less on both sides. The *Prime Minister* found himself in hearty concurrence with this, and the Council agreed with the *Prime Minister*. After they had discussed their unanimity for some days, the *King* yawned and announced that he had made up his mind to go and see for himself.

The expedient is no new one: *Prince Souci* made no claim to originality. But it is sometimes the only one, and, strange to say, it not seldom succeeds.

The magnificence of an embassy must correspond, of course, with the rank of the ambassador; and so splendid an embassy as *Prince Souci's* there never was. He left his realm in charge of his *Prime Minister*, who not only answered " Ditto " to everything, but signed it (for that was his name). It is needless to say that everyone loved the worthy man in return, or that quite a large number of people consulted him upon their affairs with the simple object of hearing him agree with them. It is possible—though not easy, perhaps—to have a worse Prime Minister than *Ditto*.

Prince Souci arrived at the *Princess Diaphanie's* court, and was received no less magnificently than he came. After the first audience he proposed a second and private one, " being afraid," as he very politely put it, " that, where first impressions were so dazzling, there must surely be some illusion, and he wished to render the exactest account to the king, his master."

(Of course, though everybody pretended not to know it, everybody knew perfectly well that the ambassador was *Prince Souci* himself and no other. But nothing pleases a Court better than a secret which is at the same time matter of public knowledge.)

To escape long ceremonies by which he was frankly bored, *Prince Souci* proposed further that the second interview should take place in the garden. The *Princess* made some difficulties about this: but seeing that the weather was perfect and the air very still, she at length consented.

Scarcely, however, had *Souci* bowed and *Diaphanie* curtseyed, before a gentle breeze blew through the garden and set the *Princess* swaying. She looked around for her attendants, but they had withdrawn out of delicacy. The *King* sprang forward to steady her. At once the wind he caused, uniting with the other, carried her farther from him. He stretched out both arms, and continued to pursue.

"Ah, *Princess!*" he cried, "surely you are not running away from me?"

"My goodness, gracious no!" she answered. "Run a little faster and catch me—I shall be ever so much obliged. . . . This is what comes," she added in a pet, "of talking in a garden! As if one couldn't talk ever so much better and more safely in a room with all the windows closed!"

Souci continued to run in chase, but the breeze ran faster still. Pf!—it rose so fast that in another moment the *Princess* was at the end of the garden and on the edge of a ha-ha, beyond which spread the open country. She cleared it like a bird: and *Souci*, following to the brink, was obliged to stop short.

"Dear, dear, dear!" he cried as he saw the lovely *Diaphanie* floating over the plain, now twirled by the wind and anon carried forward by it in short rushes—until, in less time than you can think, she had vanished out of sight.

The attendants had run meanwhile with the alarm, and within ten minutes all the Court came pouring out on foot and on horseback to the rescue of the *Princess*, who really was in no little danger; for the wind was gathering in force minute by minute, and ended in blowing a gale. *Souci*, left to himself on the edge of the ha-ha, slowly retraced his steps, reflecting as he went on the extreme volatility of the proposed bride, and how inconvenient—nay, how ridiculous—it would be to possess a wife who rose to the least wind like a kite. On reaching the palace he ordered his suite to pack at once, and was himself mounting to depart at the very moment when they brought back the *Princess* in a well-closed coach. She had been found two leagues away, wet to the skin, and blown against a haystack which by good fortune intercepted her flight. *Souci*, unwilling to incommode her, and feeling sure she must be in a hurry to get into dry clothes, stayed but to send his compliments on her escape, and rode away for home.

This adventure made him more than a little cross. To add to his vexation, when he reached home he could not but be aware (for he was by no means a fool) that his courtiers and court ladies were making bad jokes about it behind his back. In disgust at being surrounded by a crowd of people who put a dozen different clever constructions upon the simplest action, he resolved to set off on fresh travels and to journey alone—or to be accurate, with a single squire, whom he very soon managed to lose.

Yet the loss, though by contrivance, was none of his contriving. It happened in this way.

Having set his horse's head for the north-east—in the direction precisely opposite to that of his previous embassy—he rode and rode until he crossed the borders of his own kingdom and found himself in one over which the *Fairy Aveline* held sway as regent for her god-daughter, the orphaned *Princess Minon-Minette*.

Now as the *Fairy Girouette* had brought up *Souci*, so

the *Fairy Aveline* had brought up *Minon-Minette*, but with a steadier purpose. Sons must be left, after their training, to take their own line, but a mother's first and last and steadiest purpose is to find a good husband for her daughter; and for *Minon-Minette* the *Fairy Aveline* was as provident as for a real daughter. Years ago, when the *Princess* was but an infant, *Aveline* had started to make enquiries, and had, in her own mind, fixed upon *Souci* as the likeliest husband for her dear ward. She had never broached the subject seriously to the *Fairy Girouette*, because *Girouette* could never be trusted to carry out any settled purpose. She was well aware, too—having kept herself informed—that *Souci* had been ill-educated. Nevertheless, all reports agreed that he was of a good disposition and might, with training—though it must be severe since it came late—be turned into a paragon of princes.

The first thought, then, of the wise *Aveline*, as soon as *Souci* had crossed over the frontier of his own kingdom, was to deprive him of all that would remind him of it. To this end, during the first night's encampment, she caused his squire to wander and lose himself in the forest; and, further, while the *Prince* slept under a tree, she stole away his sword and his horse. She felt sure that, alone and thus deprived of adventitious aids, the *Prince* must declare his real self; and if the event should prove him worthy of her darling *Minon-Minette* (who, by the way, knew nothing of this scheme), why, so much the better!

When *Souci* awoke and missed his horse and his sword, he was greatly dismayed and spent a long time searching for them, until hunger—for he had no breakfast, and all his provisions were in keeping of his lost attendant—turned his thoughts in another direction, to seek for food; and off he set, almost at random.

He had walked but a very short way when he saw coming towards him a little old woman bent nearly two-double by the weight of an enormous faggot of sticks. Now the old woman was the *Fairy Aveline*, who had taken this disguise to make a trial of him. As she came close she staggered and, letting the faggot drop, had almost fallen herself when *Souci* stepped forward to steady her on her feet.

"You are ill, Dame?" he asked.

"No, I am not," said *Aveline* sharply.

"Well, I am hungry, good woman. Can you direct

me to any cottage near by, where I can find a meal?"

"No, I cannot," she answered.

"Then I wish you a very good day," said *Souci*, and was walking on, when she called after him.

"And what about my faggot? Where is you politeness, young man? Upon my word, you have been nicely brought up! What did they teach you at school?"

"Me? Why, nothing," answered *Souci*, with entire truth.

"I can quite well believe that. You don't even know how to pick up a faggot, it seems . . . Yes, you can come near: I can teach you how to pick up a faggot, and may be a thing or two besides."

Prince Souci blushed at her reproaches, for he felt that they had some truth in them. He took up the faggot without another word and swung it on to his back.

"That is better," said *Aveline*, delighted at the success of her first trial of him.

She hobbled behind, talking at a great rate, sometimes addressing him, more often muttering to herself, mumbling her words as old women do.

"A good plan," said she, "if all the kings in the world had to carry what you are carrying, once in their lives! They would learn then how much labour it costs to keeps their fires alight."

Souci had never thought of this before. "This old dame talks some sense," he told himself, and suddenly he felt compassion enter his heart for all poor toiling folk.

"This is all very well, *Goody*—but where are we going?" he asked.

"To the Castle of the *White Demon*. If you are in want of employment, I can find you work there."

"What sort of work? The employment I want just now, *Goody*, is to eat a breakfast."

"You told me a moment ago that you knew nothing: and that was true enough. But you have learnt something already. You see there is nothing like finding a task and applying oneself to it. In time you may become quite accomplished."

"Accomplished!" exclaimed *Souci*. "Upon my word, a mighty fine accomplishment—carrying a bundle of sticks!"

"No vain-glory, if you please!" the *Fairy* interrupted.

"You have a deal to learn yet. But never mind: you are doing a kindness to old age and an act of courtesy to womankind. Do you call that nothing for a first lesson?"

Prince Souci, to tell the truth, received these commendations somewhat impatiently. He was ready to drop under the weight of his load, and in fact was on the the point of casting it down to ease his back and take a rest, when a young damsel appeared at a turning of the path and came running towards them. She was more beautiful than the day, and her dress sparkled all over with diamonds.

"You dear thing!" she cried as she ran to the old woman. "I knew you would be tiring yourself, and was just coming to see if I could help you."

"Here is a young man," replied the old woman, "who will make no difficulty about handing you over his load. You see how sulky he looks at having to carry it."

"Will you let me take it, sir?" asked the maiden prettily.

Souci's honour was piqued. He thanked her, but clung to his faggot, which he gripped more tightly, and indeed it seemed lighter now as the three walked on together. But this, I think, must have been an illusion due to the presence of the *Princess*, in whom he discovered a fresh charm at every step.

At the same time his vanity—call it childish if you will—made him anxious not to be mistaken for a mere carrier of faggots: though he was so clumsy at the work that he might have spared himself this anxiety. To create a good impression he began to narrate the theft of his horse and sword: he mentioned carelessly the number of servants he kept: but something restrained him from talking about his rank and his kingdom.

All this, too, he might have forborne. Neither the *Princess* nor the old woman seemed to be listening with any attention. Thus they walked on together until they reached the Castle, which struck him as a fine country-house, neatly situated but with nothing extraordinary about it. They showed him where to put down his bundle in the back courtyard; and *Souci*, possessed with a false shame lest it should be discovered that he—a king—had made so undignified an entry, would have bowed and taken his leave at once had not the recollection of the *Princess's* charms kept him lingering.

For *Minon-Minette* and the old woman had entered the house without offering him any hospitality or indeed taking any notice of him.

There he was left, feeling somewhat lonely and very much of a fool, until at length a footman came out and asked if he would be pleased to rest himself in the drawing-room. *Souci* followed the man, and found himself in a charming room, bright with sunshine and crowded everywhere with books, instruments of music, masks and fancy dresses. He found a window-seat and picked up a book: but he had scarcely read a couple of lines before the door opened, and in walked, by twos and threes, a number of guests who chatted and trifled together in groups, or dispersed, one to take up a guitar, another to touch a harpsichord, a third and fourth to play at trying on masks,—all without saying a word to *Souci*, or at the best acknowledging his presence with the very coldest of bows.

Nor did matters improve when *Minon-Minette* made her appearance, surrounded by a still more brilliant and distinguished company. *Souci*, from his window-seat, could hear and follow their sallies of wit, and felt a great desire to join in their conversation, which nevertheless he knew to be too clever for him: but still no one paid him the smallest attention.

Hard as this was to be endured by a young monarch who had known nothing but flattery from his cradle up, it became yet harder when a major-domo announced that dinner was served, and he observed of a sudden that several eyes were turned on him curiously, and that the guests, sinking their voices, were evidently weighing the chances of this stranger's being admitted to dine with them.

Minon-Minette, however, cut short this discussion by making a sign to him—it was the first sign that she was aware of his presence—to follow the guests into the dining hall, where she turned and said, coldly enough,—"There is your place, sir"—indicating a seat at the lower end of the table.

Souci took it without remonstrance. By this time he was becoming accustomed to humiliations, and a growing sense of his own shortcomings obliged him to admit to himself that—his rank apart—he had no claim to a higher seat in this company. For, as the conversation grew animated, he became more and more painfully convinced that never in his life could he hope, on his own merits, to claim any place amid such wit and talent.

To his credit he did not attempt to appear cleverer than he was: but contented himself with making, as occasion offered, a remark or two which at least carried evidence of good temper and good sense. The ladies to the right and left of him capped these remarks easily and pleasantly enough. Indeed (and this was the astonishing thing) as amid all the luxury at this table there was never a trace of bad taste, so amid all the wit there was never a trace of malice.

But as *Minon-Minette*, towards whom he found his gaze constantly turning, made more and more impression on his heart, more and more *Souci* realised how desperate and even absurd was his passion. These friends of hers totally eclipsed him. He would have given worlds to be able to say something original, arresting: but to his credit he was not foolish enough to try.

After dinner there was much music and singing, and again he blushed to himself for his ignorance of these arts. Yesterday he had imagined himself a fine fellow, not without accomplishments. To-day he knew only that he knew nothing; and with the shame of this discovery mingled the diffidence of an unregarded lover. For by this time he was over head and ears in love, and *Minon-Minette* seemed to have forgotten his presence! During the concert she never once cast him a look.

He could bear it no longer, but slipped to the door and stole away down to the garden, where he wasted a whole hour in gazing at the moon, heaving prodigious sighs, cursing his fate, forming a hundred resolutions to depart and learn to forget. (But this, he foresaw, would take a very long time.) Finally, in despair, he went in search of the old woman. If she could not teach him to be clever and self-confident, to vie with these rivals, he could at least have the pleasure of talking about *Minon-Minette*.

He found her in a basement chamber, spinning—or rather, winding her distaff.

"Eh! is that you?" said the old dame, peering at him and blinking. "So they asked you to dinner, did they? Not a bad reward, I must say, for carrying a faggot! Well, and how did you get on?"

"None too well," answered *Souci*. "But if you please, *Goody*, let us talk about *Minon-Minette*. She is so beautiful" he sighed; "that doubtless all who see her are in love with her. How can they help it?"

"So much the worse for them," said the *Fairy Aveline* smiling, "unless she loves in return."

"And no doubt," went on *Souci* dejectedly, "all my rivals in the drawing-room are either kings or heirs-apparent to some throne or other, or princes of the blood-royal at the very least."

"Not a bit of it," answered the *Fairy*. "On the contrary, quite a number of them are simple gentlemen, elevated by talent or merit to be a match for royalty itself."

"I think," said *Souci* in his simplicity, "that these must be the most dangerous of all."

Again *Aveline* smiled. "Nevertheless," she said, "*Minon-Minette* will marry a king. It matters not how powerful a king, if only he be amiable enough to touch her heart."

"You bid me despair," said poor *Souci*. "But yet I shall go on loving her. My rank, dignities, self-esteem—all these I feel to be as nothing. I will sacrifice them all, and gladly, if only by losing them I can repair what I lack and make myself agreeable in her eyes. Tell me, good dame, what she would prize most in a lover? Alas! it is some accomplishment, I fear. And I have none."

"Talents and accomplishments amuse her, to be sure," replied the good dame, "but the lover who would touch her heart must touch it by his own natural self. There is no other way. . . . Take my advice, with my thanks for your confidence, and go back to the drawing-room."

"You have been extremely kind," said *Souci*, "in allowing me to inflict my troubles upon you. Will it repay your patience if I bring you in your faggot of sticks every day?"

"It is enough," said *Aveline*, "that in your trouble you remembered good manners and made that offer to an old woman. Your education is advancing rapidly. And now take this," she added, holding out a ball of thread. "One of these days you may find it useful."

"This old lady is much less disagreeable than I thought her this morning," said *Souci* to himself: "but, all the same, she must be doting. What earthly use can a ball of thread be to me?"

Aveline, if she read his thoughts, concealed her penetration. "When this thread shall have lost its power and virtue," she went on, "your troubles will be at an end."

"It is the thread of my life, then?" said *Souci*.

"It is the thread of your love's disaster," said she.

So he took it, and went back to the drawing-room with the ball in his pocket. The guests were still there, conversing as brilliantly as ever, and only pausing in their talk as one or another was called upon to play or sing or recite or give some other exhibition of talent.

It bored *Souci* extremely: for in his jealousy he could give no attention to the performances, each new one more admirable than the last. At length a lady turned to him and said:

"But what can you do, Mr. ——? Excuse me, I did not catch your name just now."

"It is *Souci*," he answered wildly; "a ridiculous name—is it not, madam? And I can do nothing—*nothing—NOTHING!*"

Casting both hands to his head, he fled from the room and out into the garden again: from the garden to the park: from the park to the wild country beyond. He knew not whither he went; he was conscious only of having utterly disgraced himself: and he sought only to kill the pain at his heart. So, for the present, we will leave him.

* * * * *

The *Princess Minon-Minette*, if she observed his hurried—and it must be admitted, unconventional—retreat from the drawing-room, went on talking quite as if nothing had happened. By and by her guests took their departure: and I own to some doubt if these extremely witty and fascinating guests were real persons after all and not apparitions created by the *Fairy Aveline* for her own purposes. Be that as it may, they took their departure: and on the morrow the *Fairy* conveyed *Minon-Minette* back to her capital, after shutting up the country house, on leaving it, in the most convenient way—that is, by a simple wave of the wand.

Important business called them.

To understand it we must visit a third kingdom and make acquaintance with a third fairy—the *Fairy Grimace*.

This third kingdom, which lay to the north-west of *Souci's*, was ruled over by *Prince Fluet*, a young man of about the same age of *Souci*—that is to say, of an age to choose himself a wife. His godmother *Grimace*, in the course of her enquiries, had happened to pay a call on our old friend *Girouette*; and *Girouette*, who never stopped to think or to consult her books, but let her tongue run away with her, promptly began to chat of the wonderful reports that had reached her concerning the wit and beauty of *Minon-Minette*: with the result that *Grimace* determined on the spot to secure this paragon for her prince. Accordingly she wrote a letter announcing that she would do herself the honour of paying the *Fairy Aveline* a visit; and that is why *Aveline* and *Minon-Minette* hurried back to the capital from their country house.

Grimace arrived, then, to be received in state, with all the ceremony due from one distinguished fairy to another: and next morning *Fluet* was presented. *Minon-Minette* found him good-looking enough, but effeminate; and in fact he was, or thought himself, so delicate that the least over-exertion in singing or dancing laid him up for days together.

I think, between ourselves, that *Minon-Minette* had already lost a little piece of her heart to the absent *Souci*. At any rate she showed some impatience with *Fluet's* headaches and vapours and nervous breakdowns—the rather that she could detect in him, apart from the tender consideration for himself, nothing deep at all. His manners struck her as mincing, as his accomplishments were plainly of the pettiest.

After some days *Prince Fluet*—who, it scarcely needs to be said, had fallen in love after his fashion—finding that he made no headway, accused *Minon-Minette* of trifling with his affection and indulged in such a storm of reproaches that he had to take to his bed for a week. *Grimace*, gravely concerned for her pet—her fears, indeed, painted this latest malady as likely to be mortal—very soon discovered what had happened, and sought out *Aveline* in a fury of a temper.

"This precious pupil of yours is a coquette, an affected minx! She thinks of nothing but herself from morning to night, as if the whole world were made to go wild over her airs and graces! She has trifled with the heart of my darling *Fluet*. I have come to tell you, Madam, that she does not trifle with *me!*"

Thereupon *Grimace* swore by her one remaining tooth—a terrible oath—that *Minon-Minette* should never know happiness until she had found—what think you?—

A bridge without an arch and a bird without a feather.

The old fairy gabbled so furiously, and made such faces as she choked over her rage, that the good *Aveline* scarcely understood her. She might have been alarmed, indeed, had she heard the explosion of rage an hour later, when *Grimace* in her private room discovered by her arts that *Minon-Minette* was already half in love with *Prince Souci.* As it was, she received with tranquillity the message that her guests had cut short their visit, and answered with a few expressions of polite regret.

* * * * *

Meanwhile *Souci* had more than once reproached himself for his hasty flight; indeed, he reproached himself whenever he thought of *Minon-Minette*, which was a thousand times a day. Yet he had too much self-respect to turn back—for self-respect goes deeper than self-esteem—and held on his way with fortitude, having by *Aveline's* arts recovered his horse and sword, which he found together in the clearing where during his sleep he had lost them.

Beyond the forest lay a desert, and beyond this, a

second desert. He crossed them and came to a country which, even from a distance, he perceived to be inhabited. But scarcely had he taken a step over the frontier before a company of soldiers sprang upon him and made him their prisoner. Having bound him hand and foot, they proceeded to carry him to the capital.

"But I have done no wrong," he protested; "Why are you treating me like this?"

His guards merely answered that he was in the territory of the *Iron King*, and seemed to consider this a sufficient explanation. They led him into the presence of that monarch, who was seated on a black throne in a hall draped with black, as a token of mourning for the numerous relatives he had put to death.

"Young man," said the *Iron King* sternly; "what are you doing in my country?"

"I came here by accident," answered *Souci*. "Moreover, if I ever escape from your abominable kingdom, I will take warning by you and treat my own subjects differently."

"Ha! I perceive that I have caught a game-cock," said the *Iron King*. His demeanour changed of a sudden, and stepping down from his throne he offered *Souci* his hand. "You are a brave fellow," said he, "and for a long time I have found no one so worthy of my friendship."

But *Souci*, irritated by his bonds and the indignity of being carried like a trussed fowl, rejected the proffered hand.

"I want none of your friendship," he answered; "Kings ought to set a good example, which you are very far from doing; and I tell you plainly, lest by keeping silence I might seem to approve of your conduct."

It must be allowed that this little lecture of *Souci's* was a trifle priggish, and moreover out of place. But youth is not always tactful, and our *Prince* (as we know) had still a great deal to learn.

At any rate, it annoyed the *Iron King* excessively.

"To be insulted thus in my own Court!" he cried with an oath. "This is too much. Away with him to the Bijou!"

Now this Bijou, as he facetiously called it, was an iron cage suspended by four thick chains from the vaulted roof of a dungeon. The prisoner could neither lie down in it nor stand upright, and by a nice arrangement of draughts and furnaces the temperature was made to alternate between icy cold and intolerable heat. In this cage, then, the guards deposited *Souci* and locked him safe with a hundred ingenious bolts.

Girouette, who ought all this while to have been looking after her godson, had almost forgotten his existence in the chase after some new idea. 'Out of thought' with her was 'out of mind,' and it would have gone hard with *Souci* had not *Aveline* come to the rescue. The poor prisoner was no sooner left alone than she contrived that a voice should reach him, and in the very tone which he recognised as that of his adored *Minon-Minette*.

"The Ball of Thread!" it whispered softly.

His heart leapt at the sound, and he took the ball from his pocket, though unable to imagine how it could help him. "For what is a thread useful? Why, for for tying, to be sure," he reflected, and half idly he tied the end to one of the bars of his cage and gave a pull on it. To his astonishment the iron broke in two without the smallest resistance.

It cost *Souci* a very little time, you may be sure, to cut his way out of the cage, and scarcely longer to deal in like manner with the iron window-gratings of the dungeon. But his heart sank when he perceived that the courtyard beyond was surrounded by an immensely high wall, smooth as glass, without a crevice into which he could put so much as the point of a toe. He saw no prospect now save of being caught and led back to a horrible death: for the *Iron King* would be furious on learning of his prisoner's escape and of the damage done to his Bijou.

But though he must die, he resolved that at any rate the good dame's gift should not fall into the *Iron King's* hands to profit such a tyrant. So he tossed it over the wall, at the same time exclaiming "Lady, I am more unfortunate than you are powerful! I thank you and restore your gift."

But the ball, as it flew, unravelled itself and let drop a trail of thread close to *Souci's* hand. He clutched the end of it. At the same moment he felt a jerk, and lo! the thread had hitched across the coping of the wall. *Souci* tugged once or twice, but it could not be dislodged, nor yet did it break.

"Surely so thin a thread cannot bear my weight?" said he. "And yet, better trust to a thread than to the tender mercies of a King!"

He climbed it hand over hand, being young and agile, and quickly gained the top: whence he slid down like a flash to the turf, where the ball lay, on the far side. But—most singular of all, perhaps—he had no sooner picked up the ball than its tail of thread came gliding over the smooth wall like a snake, and in another instant had rewound itself in his hand.

Souci blessed the fairy, and, pocketing the ball, ran off at his best speed; for a great beating of drums within the castle warned him that the guards had discovered the broken cage, and he must put as much space as possible between him and the *Iron King's* vengeance. He soon came to a broad river, and here again he was almost in despair of crossing, for it was too broad to swim and the current ran swiftly.

But again he seemed to hear *Minon-Minette's* voice reminding him "The Thread—try the Ball of Thread!"—and the thread, when he flung it, made as good a bridge as it had formerly made a ladder.

Yet another fright, however, awaited him; for on reaching the farther shore, he espied a great army marching along the bank towards him, with standards and ensigns flying. His first thought was that this army must belong to the *Iron King*, and had been sent to cut off his escape. But crouching behind some bushes he perceived, as the army approached, that the device on its standard was the same—a Winged Heart—that he had seen on the flag above *Minon-Minette's* country house; and to put the question beyond doubt, the soldiers were dressed in the *Princess's* colours, of pale blue and rose.

Prince Souci ran forward, and threw himself before the vanguard. "A moment!" he cried. "Do these troops belong to the *Princess Minon-Minette?*"

The captain of the vanguard reined up his horse, and the whole troop halted. "They do," said he; "and what is more, we are marching at her orders to avenge the treatment offered to *Your Majesty* by the *Iron King.*"

"She knows of my rank, then?" thought *Souci.* But after all (he reflected) there was nothing so marvellous in this. The old dame, who could perform such wonders with a ball of thread, might easily have divined his secret and told the *Princess.* The real marvel—and almost too good to be true—was that *Minon-Minette* should take such an interest in his fate!

"Where is your mistress, that I may thank her?"

"Alas, sire!" answered the officer dolefully, "we would that we knew! Two days ago by the borders of the The Three Kingdoms she rode ahead of the army and has never ridden back. We thought to overtake her by the borders of this river: but we march in vain. It is feared that she has fallen into the hands of the *Iron King*.

* * * * *

But she had not. You shall now hear what had happened.

The *Fairy Aveline*, when *Minon-Minette* announced her intention of riding at the head of the army, had allowed her to go, but with many misgivings; which were the livelier since by this time the brave girl made no secret of her attachment to *Souci*, and had taken to follow the chase, spending many hours daily in the saddle, the better to inure herself to the rigours of a campaign. At parting, the fairy—who was to follow in a coach—implored her to be careful of one thing above all others. "Never cross the borders of your own country until you come to that of the *Iron King;* and—for my coach is slow and will lag behind the army—

remember this especially when I am not near to protect you."

The *Princess* promised readily enough to observe this advice; but one day as she was riding along on her beautiful white hackney, thinking a good deal about her beloved *Souci* and not at all about the frontiers of her realm (of which, indeed, she had no exact knowledge), she found herself of a sudden in front of a hut which seemed to be built entirely of dry leaves. The aspect of it was strangely sinister; and as *Aveline's* warning crossed her mind she attempted to turn the hackney about. But it stood there as if rooted. The *Princess* felt an invisible force which, against her will, compelled her to dismount and walk towards the cottage.

As she approached it the door opened, and *Grimace* appeared on the threshold.

"So here you are at last, fair *Minon-Minette*! I have had my trap set for you this long while. Step inside, my pretty! Eh? I am going to teach you to make war on my friends. Things will not turn out as you expected, I promise. I take some pleasure in talking to you of this *Iron King*, because before long you will have to go on your knees to him and not only beg his pardon for daring to march an army against him, but implore him to do you the honour of marrying you. In the meantime, understand, if you please, that you are my servant!"

The evil *Grimace* was as good—rather, as bad—as her word. Forthwith she put poor *Minon-Minette* to the meanest tasks. Her dinner was black bread, her bed a pallet of straw. In the morning, to expose her to the worst heat of the day, *Grimace* sent her out to look after the geese; and no doubt that day *Minon-Minette* would have suffered a sunstroke if she had not happened in the field upon—of all strange things to find lying in a field—a beautiful fan.

Minon-Minette wasted little time in wondering how it came there, but picked it up and opened it, to shield her face from the noon-day heat. If a fan went oddly with a goose-girls's occupation, why, so did her fine clothes. But as she opened it out dropped a letter. It ran:—

"I have passed this way, and I am always seeking you.

"*Souci.*"

Then *Minon-Minette* was comforted a little; for she thought that if *Souci* had passed that way, seeking her, by the same road sooner or later he might return.

She used the dear fan all that day to shield her from the sun, and the next day, and the next. At the end of a week *Grimace*, astonished to find that the *Princess* still kept her clear rose-and-white colour, began to watch her narrowly; and came upon her in the act of drawing a fan from the bosom of her bodice; for to *Minon-Minette* the fan was serviceable, indeed, yet by this time not one half so serviceable as it was dear.

"Give me that fan!" cried *Grimace*, trying to snatch it from her.

"I would sooner give you my life!" answered *Minon-Minette*, summoning up all her courage: and to save it from *Grimace's* clutch she put it beneath her feet and stood on it firmly.

She had no sooner done so than she felt herself lifted from the ground; and while *Grimace* stood and worked her face with fury, *Minon-Minette* sailed up into air and away beyond her power.

* * * * *

Meanwhile *Souci*, finding no one in the army who could give him any news of his beloved, left it to follow its march and ran forward madly, seeking her all over the wide world. "Since there is no news of her on earth," cried he, at length, "can there be any in the sky?" For he had again remembered his ball of thread.

Snatching it from his pocket, he hurled it with all his force up towards the sky.

He had never flung it so far. Up it flew, and still up, until the very heart of the ball was unravelled; and out from the heart broke and flew, still soaring aloft, a little naked *Cupid*.

Aloft, after him, still clutching at the end of his thread, was borne *Prince Souci*. He shortened-in the length of it, climbing much as he had climbed over the wall, until at length he found himself with a short rein, driving the winged boy, who still flew forward.

Then, at length—at length!—a speck appeared, far away in the sky. It grew larger.

Behold! it was *Minon-Minette*, sliding, swooping towards him on her fan!

"They are met!" she cried with a gay laugh, as they encountered and passed and turned again, circling still nearer and nearer.

"*What* are met, O Beloved?" asked *Souci*, though

he could hardly make himself heard for the rush of wind and of his emotion.

"Why, the bird without feathers and the bridge without an arch!"

Below was the army battering down the *Iron King's* citadel; but this military success scarcely mattered to the happiness of *Souci* and *Minon-Minette* as their two equipages, the fan and *Cupid*, drew close, and they exchanged their first kiss—in mid-air.

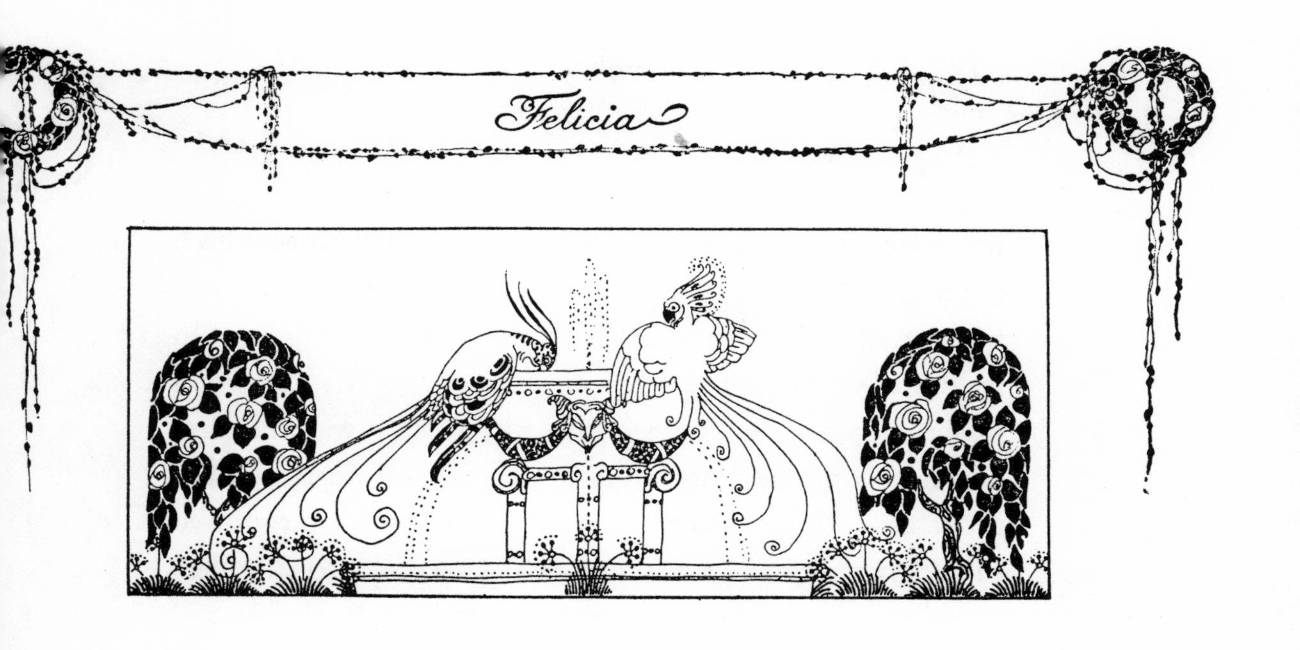

FELICIA

OR

THE POT OF PINKS

ONCE upon a time a poor labourer, falling sick and knowing himself to be on the point of death, called to his bedside his son and daughter—both of whom he loved tenderly—and divided his few belongings between them.

"Your poor dear *Mother*," said he, "brought to me for dowry two stools and a straw mattress. I possess, moreover, a hen, a pot of pinks, and a silver ring, which were given me by a great lady who once did me the honour to lodge for a night in my lowly cottage. On leaving she said to me, ‘ Despise not these gifts, my good man: be careful to keep the pinks well watered and never to lose the ring. As for your daughter, she shall grow up to be the loveliest in the land. I charge you to call her *Felicia* and, when she grows up, to give her the ring and the pinks to console her for her poverty.' Take them both, then, my dearest *Felicia*," said the dying man, "and your brother *Beddo* shall have everything else."

The two children seemed content with this. When their father was dead, they mourned for him and divided his possessions as he had willed, without dispute. *Felicia* believed that her brother loved her; but when she took one of the stools, to sit down upon it, he said to her churlishly:

" Keep your pot of pinks and your ring, but let my stools alone. I like order in my house."

Felicia, who was very gentle, fell to weeping quietly. She made no answer, but remained standing while *Beddo* sat at his ease. Supper time came and *Beddo* had a nice fresh egg. He ate it and threw the shell to his sister.

"There!" he said. "That is all I can spare for you. If you don't like it, run out and catch frogs: there are plenty in the marsh close by."

Still *Felicia* did not answer him. But she wept more sadly than ever, and by-and-by crept away to her little room.

She found it filled with a delicious fragrance. Not doubting that this came from her pinks, she went up to them and said sadly:

"Dear pinks—you who are so sweet and pretty and my only solace now—do not fear but that I will water you well and suffer no cruel hand to tear you from your stems!" At the same time, stooping over them, she seemed to perceive that the earth in the pot was dry, and that they needed water. So taking her pitcher she ran out in the clear moonlight to the fountain, which was some distance away.

When she reached the well she was out of breath—so fast had she run; and naturally enough she sat down upon the stone brink to rest herself for a moment. But hardly had she done so when she perceived a stately lady advancing towards her in the moonlight, attended by a company of guards in liveries of amaranth velvet, embroidered with pearls, and by eight maids-of-honour, of whom one walked at her either hand while the remaining six held up the train of her robe.

Other servants followed, bearing a canopy which they erected beside the fountain, and a sofa of cloth-of-gold whereon the lady reclined while they served her with the daintiest of suppers from a table covered with golden dishes and goblets of crystal. Lutes were brought, and their music with the tinkling murmur of the fountain made accompaniment to an invisible chorus that softly chanted :—

> List, ah, list to the zephyr in the grove !
> Where beneath the happy boughs
> Flora builds her summerhouse :
> Whist ! ah, whist ! while the cushat tells his love,
> Tells it twenty times and over.
> To remind a human lover
> He has kiss'd—once kiss'd—for a seal on silly vows !

Felicia beheld these marvels in the moonlight, peeping through a bush behind which she had concealed herself, scarcely venturing to move. But after a few moments the *Queen* said to one of her guards :

Princess Diaphanie walks with her attendants.

MINON-MINETTE

Page 18

"Ah, Princess!" he cried. "Surely you are not running away from me?"

MINON-MINETTE

Page 21

Prince Fluet had to take to his bed for a week.

MINON-MINETTE

Page 39

"Young man," said the Iron King sternly, "what are you doing in my country?"

MINON-MINETTE

Page 41

Princess Minon-Minette searches for Prince Souci.

MINON-MINETTE

Page 48

Princess Minon-Minette and Prince Souci exchange their first kiss.

MINON-MINETTE

Page 52

List, ah, list to the zephyr in the grove!

FELICIA

Page 56

Felicia salutes the Queen of the Woods with a graceful curtsey.

FELICIA

Page 57

"I fancy you will find a shepherdess hidden yonder. Bid her come forward."

Felicia thereupon stepped forth and, terrified though she was, saluted the *Queen* respectfully; with so graceful a curtsey, indeed, that all stood astonished as she went on to lift the edge of the royal train to her lips and so stood upright, lowering her eyes modestly. A rosy blush showed on the moon-lit white of her cheek; the prettiest commingling of ardour and innocence.

"What are you doing here, pretty child?" asked the *Queen*. "Are you not afraid of robbers?"

"Alas! madam," answered *Felicia*. "What could any robbers hope to gain from a poor shepherdess who has only a frock of coarse linen?"

"You are not very rich, then?" asked the *Queen*, smiling.

"I am so poor," replied *Felicia*, "that a pot of pinks and a silver ring are all my worldly goods."

"But you have a heart?" said the *Queen*. "If anyone wanted to steal that, would you give it to him?"

"I do not know what you mean, madam, or how it is possible to give one's heart. I have always heard tell that without a heart no-one can live, and if it is broken one dies; and, poor though I am, it seems to me good to live."

"Quite right, my dear!" said the *Queen*. "Always be sure to take care of your heart. But tell me, pretty one, have you supped?"

"Very poorly, madam," answered *Felicia*. Indeed, my brother *Beddo* ate up all there was."

The *Queen* thereupon ordered that a place should be made for her at table, and herself would have loaded her with the best of good cheer. But poor *Felicia* was so much overcome with astonishment that she could scarcely swallow a morsel.

"I want to know, my dear," said the *Queen* by-and-by, "what you were doing at the fountain so late?"

"Madam, I came but to fetch a pitcher of water for my pinks." Here *Felicia* stooped to pick up the pitcher at her side, when to her amazement she found it turned to gold, glittering all over with diamonds, and filled with water which smelt deliciously.

"But this cannot belong to me!" stammered poor *Felicia*.

"Yes, it is yours," said the *Queen*. "Go, child;

water your pinks with it; and remember that the *Queen of the Woods* is your friend."

At these words the shepherdess threw herself at the *Queen's* feet.

"Ah, madam," she cried. "You do me so much kindness! Deign only to wait here a moment while I run and fetch my pot of pinks to you. They are the half of all I possess, and they could be in no better hands than yours!"

"Go *Felicia*," said the *Queen*, stroking her cheek softly; "I promise to wait here until you return."

Felicia picked up her golden pitcher, and ran with it to her little room. But whilst she had been away her brother *Beddo* had gone in and taken the pot of pinks, leaving a great cabbage in its place. When her eyes fell on this unlucky cabbage, *Felicia* was greatly distressed and scarcely knew what to do. But at length she summoned up courage to run back to the fountain, where she cast herself on her knees before the *Queen*.

"Madam," cried she, "my brother *Beddo* has stolen my pot of pinks; and now there is nothing left to me but my ring. Accept that, I beg of you, as a token of my gratitude.

"But if I take your ring, pretty shepherdess," said the *Queen*, "you are left portionless."

"Ah, madam," replied *Felicia* with the most winning of smiles, "so long as I possess your good graces how can I be portionless?"

The *Queen* took the ring and slipped it upon her finger. Thereupon, mounting her chariot, which was of coral studded with emeralds, she shook rein to the six milk-white horses that awaited her command, and was borne away. *Felicia* gazed after her until the chariot disappeared in the moonlight at a parting of the forest glades, and so went back, wondering, to the cottage.

The first thing she did on entering her room was to pick up the cabbage and throw it out of the window.

But she was very much astonished, as she threw it, to hear a voice cry out—and seemingly from the heart of the cabbage—

"Oh dear, dear, dear! This will be the death of me!" —because in a general way cabbages do not speak.

As soon as it was daylight, *Felicia*, still distressed at the loss of her pot of pinks, went out to look for it, and the first thing she happened on was the unfortunate cabbage. She gave it a sharp push with her foot, saying:

"What are you doing here?—you who dared to thrust yourself into my room, in the place of my pinks! Is this some more of your meddling?"

"Who wanted to be in your room?" answered the *Cabbage* in an aggrieved voice. "You may be sure I had never entered it without being carried."

Again it gave her a little thrill of fright to hear a cabbage talk: but he went on—

"If you will kindly take me back and plant me among my companions again, I will tell you in half a dozen words where to find your pinks. They are hidden under *Beddo's* bed."

Felicia was in despair on hearing this, for she knew not how to recover them. But she planted the cabbage back in its place very carefully, and then, catching sight of her brother's hen that was following her and pretending to scratch up the earth, she turned about quickly and took hold of it by the neck, crying:

"Wretched bird, I believe you are at the bottom of this mischief! I have a good mind to make you pay for all my brother's unkindness!"

"K'k! k'k! k'k!—please, shepherdess, don't choke me!" gasped the hen; "I am a terrible gossip—I confess it; but if only you will let me go I can tell you such a story!"

"Tell it, then," said *Felicia*.

"K'k! k'k! Oh! my poor throat! Let me tell you, then, deary, that you are not the daughter of the poor peasant by whom you were brought up. No; your mother was a *Queen* who had six daughters before you were born, and—as if it were her fault, poor lady!—the King her husband threatened to kill her unless her next child should be a son and heir: and she was shut within a tower, with sentries set to guard her until her next child was born—and she, too, turned out to be a little Princess.

"But in the meantime the good *Queen* had managed to get a letter conveyed to her sister, who was a fairy, and who happened not long before to have given birth to a fairy Prince. This good Fairy, on her sister's supplication, placed her own babe in a cradle of roses and gave command to the zephyrs to carry him to the tower. But I think they must have dallied by the way. At any rate the *Queen*, getting no news, prevailed on one of her guards, whose heart melted with pity at her sad extremity, to let her escape from the tower by means of a rope ladder, carrying you—a day-old babe—in her arms. Her only thought was to hide you from your pursuers; and at length, half dead with hunger and fatigue, she dragged herself to this cottage in the woods. I was the labourer's wife," said the hen, "and I made a good nurse, though I say it! The good *Queen* at any rate gave you into my keeping, and told me all her trouble; and then she died, poor dear lady, without time to tell us what was to be done with you.

"The best in my power I did for you, too, deary. But lack-a-daisy! in all my life I could no more help chattering than I can help cackling now when I have laid an egg. I ran around and told the tale to my neighbours: and one day, when a beautiful lady happened to visit my cottage, I told it all to her, too; whereupon she touched me with her walking-stick and turned me into a hen—and there I was, unable to tell anything; able only to cackle, cackle, cackle! My distress was the worse, because my husband, who was at work in the fields when this misfortune overtook me, never knew what had happened, nor what had become of me. After searching everywhere he could only conclude that I had been drowned or that some wild beast had made a prey of me.

"The same great lady visited the cottage again, where he sat in his affliction. He had not recovered himself sufficiently to attend to your christening. She commanded him to call you Felicia, and left him the ring and the pot of pinks to be given to you. But while she was in the house there arrived twenty-five of the guards sent by the King, your father, to seek you out. They had been drawn to the cottage by the reports my unhappy tongue had spread; and what would have happened to you there's no guessing if she had not waved her wand again and turned them all into cabbages! It was one of them you threw out of the window last night."

"Poor fellow!" said *Felicia*. "Although he meant me ill, I can't help feeling sorry for him. It must be detestable to be a cabbage, when one has been a guardsman."

"I don't know," said the hen, "how he came to recover his speech—or, for that matter, how I recovered mine; though, thank Heaven! I have always been able to cackle. I think something must be going to happen."

Felicia was no little astonished to hear this story, and to learn that she was indeed a Princess. But she had sufficient command of herself to say:

"Pardon me, my good nurse, for having handled you so roughly. I am truly sorry, since it displeases you, that you should be a hen just now, and I wish I could see some way to remedy it. But I quite agree with you that something must be going to happen. In the meantime, however, I must go and look after my pinks; for I love them beyond anything in the world."

Now *Beddo* had gone off into the woods, never dreaming that *Felicia* would guess where the pinks were hidden: and she, delighted that he was out of the way, as little dreamed that she would find any difficulty in getting them back. Judge of her horror then when, on peeping into the room, she found the bed guarded by an army of monstrous rats! There were rats in regiments, rats in battalions, with whole companies of rats flung out on either wing—that is to say, around *Beddo's* two three-legged stools—for skirmishers; while on the bed itself a host of mice formed a corps of reserve. Scarcely had *Felicia* taken a step when the whole army advanced and flung themselves about her ankles, biting, scratching, even drawing blood: whereupon our heroine beat a hasty retreat, crying out:

"My pinks! My dear pinks! How can you stay here in such bad company?"

Then of sudden she bethought herself of the golden pitcher, and of the perfumed water which the *Queen* had given her. Might it, perhaps, possess some magic virtue to prevail against these horrible creatures? She ran, and fetching the pitcher in haste, scattered a few drops over them—when presto! their whiskers turned to tails, and the whole host bolted away for their holes in a panic.

Felicia lost no time in catching up her pot of pinks, and escaped with them almost as hastily to her own little room. She found them drooping and ready to die for want of water, and poured over them all that was left in her pitcher. Whereupon as she bent, breathing in their delicious scent, she heard a soft voice that seemed to whisper between the leaves:

"Charming *Felicia*, the day has come at last when I

may speak and tell the love your beauty inspires even in the flowers."

Felicia turned pale. Within the space of a few hours she had been addressed in human speech successively by a cabbage, a hen, and a pot of pinks, and had faced an army of rats in battle array. Overcome by these experiences she fell to the floor in a swoon.

At this moment in walked *Beddo*. Working hard in the heat of the day had somewhat affected his temper. When he saw that *Felicia* had found her pinks and recovered them from their hiding-place, he flew into a passion, dragged her—all a-swoon as she was—out into the garden, and slammed the door on her.

The fresh air revived her as she lay on the bare earth, and presently she opened her pretty eyes. There, right beside her, stood the *Queen of the Woods*; as charming and as magnificent as ever.

"You have a wicked brother," she said; "I saw how brutally he cast you out, just now. Shall I punish him as he deserves?"

"Ah, no—I pray you, madam!" answered *Felicia*, "I bear him no grudge; and if he wish ill to me, why should I imitate him?"

"But," went on the *Queen*; "what would you say if this *Beddo* were not your real brother, nor you a labourer's child after all?"

"If anyone brought that news to me," answered *Felicia* again, lowering her eyes, "I should say that it was of little account, without proof."

"What!" cried the *Queen*; "have you never heard that you were born a Princess?"

"Why to be sure, madam, I did hear some gossip to that effect this morning. But again, how should I boast of it, or even believe it, without proof?"

"Ah, dear child!" the *Queen* exclaimed. "You cannot think how I love you for your modesty. It assures me that the poverty of your upbringing has not spoilt, or even touched, the dignity of your blood. Yes, verily, you are a Princess; nor can I blame myself wholly that you have suffered so long the indignities from which I now propose to deliver you."

She was interrupted, just then, by the arrival of a young man so handsome that *Felicia* had never beheld his like. He wore a coat of green and gold silk, with buttons of emerald, and on his love-locks which fell over his shoulders rested a wreath of pink carnations.

He fell on one knee and kissed the *Queen's* hand.

"Ah!" cried she, "my son—my Pink—my beloved! The date of your enchantment is ended, then, and all by the help of this dear girl!"

Having embraced him ardently, she turned to *Felicia*.

"Charming *Princess*," said she, "I know all that the hen told you this morning. But she did not tell you—for she did not know—that the zephyrs whom I had charged to bear my infant son to your mother, arriving within sight of the tower which was her prison, laid him down in a pasture of flowers to rest while they flew ahead to tell the glad news to her.

"They meant well, no doubt. But while he lay there a fairy, with whom I had a quarrel, pounced down and changed him into a pink. It was a trick which my science might have foreseen, but could not remedy.

"I tried every art, indeed—as what mother would not, who had been robbed of a son? But still the only chance I could find was to carry *Prince Pink* to the cottage where you were brought up; in the hope that in return for your care he might grow to love you—as I believe he has. Your giving me the silver ring was the sign that the spell was weakening, that the hour of his deliverance was at hand. On the chance of frightening you by that silly army of rats my enemy staked her last throw. You beat her for me: and now, dearest *Felicia*, if with this same silver ring you can consent to wed my son, whose youth has been so unhappy—and for your sake, although you knew it not—I can promise you that so long as you live you will never regret it."

"Dear madam," answered *Felicia*, blushing, "your kindness overwhelms me. I know that you are my mother's sister, and that your heart transformed into cabbages the guards who were sent to murder me. It was you, too, who changed my chattering nurse into a hen. You do me an extreme honour in proposing that I should marry your son. But—how can I explain to you?—I know not what is in his heart—nor, indeed, what is in mine, save a feeling that it would be very delightful to be beloved, and for one's own sake."

"Speak, my son," commanded the *Queen*.

"Pardon me, mother," said the *Prince*, still kneeling, "that words come slowly to me after these years. . . . But oh! *Felicia*, if while I was dumb and a mere plant my fragrance ever spoke to you, that fragrance was my love striving to penetrate your heart. So, while you tended me, I was happy in a fashion. But did you never notice how quickly I drooped when your gentle hand ceased watering?"

"I did think it strange," confessed *Felicia*.

The *Queen* turned at once upon her and touched her with her walking-stick. The walking-stick must have been a magic wand: for on the instant *Felicia* saw her poor cotton frock changed to a robe of silver brocade embroidered with carbuncles. Over her soft dark hair fell a veil of gauze and gold, crowned with a coronet of diamonds. So queenly she appeared, yet glowing with rustic health, that *Prince Pink* cried aloud:

"*Felicia!* you, who were ever kind to me, be kind to me yet!"

"I think," said the *Queen*, smiling, while *Felicia* searched for an answer, "that your cousin will not be inexorable, dear son!"

Just then *Beddo* opened the cottage door. He was on his way back to work; but seeing the three who conversed, all so magnificently dressed, but a few yards from the threshold, he passed a hand over his brow. He supposed himself, indeed, to be dreaming.

But *Felicia* called to him quite kindly, and begged the *Queen* to have mercy on him.

"What? After all his unkindness to you?"

"Ah, madam! I am so happy! I want everyone in the world to be happy too."

The *Queen* kissed her. "Have it as you will, dear child," said she; and with a wave of her walking-stick she changed the poor hut into a palace, and *Beddo* himself felt a gush of kindness about his heart, such as he had never known before. But the two stools and the straw mattress remained in the central hall of the palace. just to remind him of his former poverty.

Then, with another wave of her walking-stick, the *Queen* stroked the cabbages, and they became guards again, and stood at attention; while the hen, whose turn came next, changed back into an old woman so rapidly that there was no knowing at what point she ceased chattering about an egg and began gossiping about her neighbours.

But the wedding of *Prince Pink* and *Princess Felicia*—so magnificent it was—kept her in talk for a whole six months; and then she was able to start upon it over again, because no one had listened to her.

THE TWELVE DANCING PRINCESSES

ONCE upon a time, in the village of Montignies-sur-Roc, there lived a little herd-boy who had lost both his father and his mother. His real name was *Michael*, but people always called him the Star-gazer, because when he drove his cows over the commons for pasture, he went along with his head in the air, staring at the sky.

Because he had a white skin, blue eyes, and hair that

curled all over his head, the village girls used to call after him, "Good-day, Star-gazer! What are you doing?" and *Michael* would answer "Eh? Nothing," and go on his way without even turning to look at them.

The truth was he thought them very ugly, with their sunburnt necks, their large red hands, their coarse petticoats and their wooden shoes. He had heard that somewhere in the world there lived maidens whose necks were white and whose hands were small, who were always dressed in fine silks and laces, and were called Princesses. So while his companions round the fire saw nothing in the flames but common everyday fancies, *Michael* dreamed that he had the happiness to marry a Princess.

II

One morning about the middle of August, just at mid-day when the sun was hottest, *Michael* ate his dinner of a morsel of dry bread, and went to sleep under an oak. While he slept, there appeared to him in a dream a beautiful lady in a robe of cloth-of-gold, who said to him:

"Go to the Castle of Bel-Œil, and there you shall marry a Princess."

That evening the little cow-boy, who had been thinking a great deal about the advice of the lady in the golden dress, told his dream to the farm people. But as was natural, they only mocked at the Star-gazer.

The next day at the same hour he went to sleep again under the shadow of the oak. The lady appeared to him a second time, and again she said:

"Go to the Castle of Bel-Œil, and you shall marry a Princess."

In the evening *Michael* told his friends that he had dreamed the same dream again. But they only mocked at him more than before.

"Never mind," he thought to himself; "if the lady appears to me a third time, I will do as she tells me."

The third day, about two o'clock in the afternoon, to the astonishment of all the village, a voice was heard singing:

> Raleô, Raleô,
> See how the cattle go!

It was the little cow-boy driving his herd back to the byre.

The farmer began to scold him, but he answered quietly: "I am going away."

So, having made up his clothes into a bundle and bidden good-bye to his friends, he set forth to seek his fortune.

There was great excitement throughout the village. The folk gathered to the top of the hill, where they held their sides with laughter to watch the Star-gazer trudging bravely along the valley, with his bundle at the end of his stick.

To be sure, it was enough to make anyone laugh.

III

It was well known for twenty miles round that there lived in the Castle of Bel-Œil twelve *Princesses* of marvellous beauty, and as haughty as they were beautiful, and moreover so delicately sensitive, by reason of their royal blood, that they would have felt at once the presence of a pea in their beds, even though twenty mattresses had been laid over it.

Gossip said too that they led just the lives that princesses ought to lead, sleeping far into the morning and never getting up before noon. They had twelve beds, all in the same room. But it was most extraordinary—

said gossip—that though they were locked in every night by triple bolts, every morning their satin shoes were found worn into holes.

When they were asked what they had been doing all night, they always answered that they had been asleep; and indeed no noise was ever heard in the room.

Yet the shoes could not wear out of themselves!

At last the *Duke of Bel-Œil* ordered a trumpet to be sounded and proclamation to be made that whoever could discover how his daughters wore out their shoes should choose one of them for his wife.

On hearing the proclamation a number of princes arrived at the castle to try their fortune. They were set, one by one, to keep sentry by the open door of the *Princesses'* room. But always the same thing happened. Always, when morning came the watcher had disappeared. and no one could tell what had become of him.

IV

When he reached the Castle of Bel-Œil, *Michael* went straight to the head gardener and asked to be taken into service. It so happened that a garden-boy had just been dismissed; and although the Star-gazer did not look very sturdy, the head-gardener agreed to take him, for he thought that the lad's handsome face and golden curls would please the *Princesses*.

The first command laid upon him was to be ready each morning with twelve bouquets, to present one to each of the *Princesses* as soon as they got up; and *Michael* thought that if he had nothing more unpleasant to do than this he should fare very well.

Accordingly next morning he took his stand outside the door of the *Princesses'* room, with twelve bouquets in a basket. When the sisters came filing forth he presented a bouquet to each. But not one, in taking it, deigned even to glance at the lad, save only *Lina* the youngest, who fixed her large dark eyes on him (they were soft as velvet, too) and exclaimed:

"Oh, how pretty he is—our new flower-boy!"

Whereat two or three of her sisters laughed: but the eldest reproved her, saying that a *Princess* ought never to lower herself so far as to take notice of a garden boy.

Now *Michael* had heard—as everyone about the Castle knew—of the proclamation, and what had befallen those who had essayed to discover the secret; how that no less than fifty *Princes* had challenged it and all had vanished without leaving a trace. Nevertheless the beautiful eyes of the *Princess Lina* inspired him with a wild longing to try his fate.

But being of so lowly a station he did not dare to offer himself, fearing that he might be turned out of the Castle for his impudence.

V

While he hesitated, the Star-gazer had another dream. The lady in the golden dress appeared to him once more. This time she held in one hand two tiny laurel trees—a cherry laurel and a rose laurel—and in the other hand a little golden rake, a little golden watering-pot and a silken towel.

"*Michael!*" said she, "Plant these two laurels in two large pots, rake them over with the rake, water them with the watering-pot, and wipe them with the towel. When they have grown as tall as a girl of fifteen, say to each of them; 'My beautiful laurel, with this golden rake I have raked you, with this golden pot I have watered you, with this silken towel I have wiped you.' Then you may ask anything you choose, and the laurels will give it to you."

Michael had just time to thank the lady before she vanished. When he awoke, he found the two plants beside him, with the rake, the watering pot, and the towel. So now he knew that his dreams were something more than dreams; and he carefully obeyed the orders which the lady had given him.

The plants grew very fast. When they were as tall as a girl of fifteen, *Michael* said to the cherry laurel:

"My beautiful laurel, with this golden rake I have raked thee, with this golden pot I have watered thee, with this silken towel I have wiped thee. Cause me now to become invisible."

Instantly there appeared on the laurel a pretty white flower. *Michael* plucked it and stuck it in his buttonhole. At once he became invisible.

VI

That same evening, when the *Princesses* went upstairs to bed, *Michael* followed them barefoot, so as to make no noise, and hid himself under one of the twelve beds.

The *Princesses* were no sooner alone (as they thought)

with the door trebly locked upon them, than in great haste they ran to their wardrobes and boxes. Out of these they took the most magnificent dresses, which they put on, turning this way and that before their mirrors, and calling on one another to adjust a jewel or a ribbon.

Michael could see nothing of this from his hiding place, but he could hear all their talk as they laughed and skipped with glee.

"Be quick, all of you!" said the eldest at length; "Our partners will be getting impatient."

By this time the Star-gazer had been in hiding for close upon an hour. The noise ceased, and he peeped out to see all the twelve sisters in splendid robes, with their satin shoes on their feet, and in their hands the bouquets he had brought them.

"Are you ready?" asked the eldest.

"Ready," responded the others in chorus, and took their places in file behind her.

The eldest *Princess* clapped her hands thrice, and a trap door opened in the floor. All the *Princesses* stepped down into a secret staircase, and *Michael* slipped after them.

He made such haste that incautiously he trod on the train of the *Princess Lina*, who was last. "Oh!" cried the *Princess Lina*, "there is somebody behind me, catching at my dress!"

"You silly!" said her eldest sister, "you are always being frightened when there is no cause. It is only a nail that hitched in your train."

VII

Down they went, down, down, until they reached a level passage, at the end of which was a door with no fastening but a latch. Their leader, the eldest *Princess*, opened it, and they passed straight into a lovely little wood, the boughs of which were powdered over with drops of silver, all liquid and sparkling in the light of the moon.

From this they passed into a second wood, where the trees glowed with gold; and thence into a third, where every small stem glittered with diamonds.

Beyond this the Star-gazer, still following the *Princesses*, came out upon the shore of a wide lake, very still beneath the moon. By the bank of the lake twelve little boats lay ready, in each of which sat a *Prince* waiting, grasping the oars. In the stern of each boat shone a lantern, beneath a silken awning.

Each *Princess* stepped into one of the boats, and *Michael* dropped into the last one, which held the youngest. The boats glided rapidly across the lake, but the *Princess Lina's* lagged farther and farther behind.

"We never went so slowly before," said the *Princess Lina;* "What can be the reason?"

"I don't know," answered her *Prince*; "I assure you I am pulling as hard as I can."

On the far side of the lake stood a castle, brilliantly illuminated from base to roof; and from it, as they approached, sounds of music greeted them—of fiddles, kettle-drums, trumpets—louder and louder.

The boats' stems grated on a beach, and all the company jumped ashore. The *Princes*, having fastened their craft, gave their arms to the *Princesses* and conducted them over the velvet lawn to the Castle.

VIII

Michael still followed them closely, and entered the ball-room in their train. Everywhere were mirrors, lights, flowers and damask hangings. The brilliance of it dazzled his eyes.

He shrank away and posted himself in a corner,

whence he could admire the dancers. Each of the *Princesses* was lovely in her different way. Some were fair and some were dark: some had auburn hair, some raven-black, some golden; and all danced divinely. But the one whom our cow-boy still thought the most adorable was the little *Princess* with the velvet eyes.

And how she danced, too!—as lightly as a leaf on the wind. Her cheeks were flushed, her eyes sparkled. Oh! it was plain that she loved dancing better than anything else.

And oh! how the poor lad envied those handsome *Princes*, in whose clasp the proud maidens danced so gracefully!

But he might have spared his envy. These partners were really the *Princes* who, to the number of fifty at least, had essayed to steal the *Princesses'* secret. The *Princesses* in return had made each of them drink of a philtre which froze the heart and left nothing but the love of dancing.

IX

They danced, and they danced, until the shoes of the *Princesses* were worn into holes. When the cock crowed a third time, the violins stopped, and a company of negro boys served a delicious supper, consisting of sugared orange-flowers, crystallised rose-leaves and violets, cracknels, wafers, and other dishes; which, as everyone knows, are the proper food to set before Princesses.

After supper the dancers all hastened back to their boats, and this time the Star-gazer entered the boat of the eldest *Princess*. They re-crossed the lake and passed again through the wood that glittered with diamonds, the wood that shone with gold, and the wood that sparkled with silver. On the edge of this last the boy tarried to break off a small branch for a souvenir. As the twig snapped, the *Princess Lina* halted and turned about.

"What was that noise?" she asked.

"It was nothing," said the eldest sister. "It was only the screech of the barn-owl that roosts in one of the castle turrets."

While they were speaking, *Michael* managed to slip in front, and running up the stairway he reached the *Princesses'* room well ahead of them. He flung open the window and, sliding down the vine which climbed up the wall, found himself in the garden just as the sun was beginning to rise and it was time to get to his work.

X

When he made up the bouquets that morning *Michael* hid the branch with the silver drops in the nosegay which he presented to the youngest *Princess*.

She was surprised and a little dismayed when she discovered it. However, she said nothing to her sisters; but later in the day, happening to meet the boy as she was walking pensively in the shade of the elms, she stopped as if to speak to him; then, altering her mind, went on her way.

That evening the twelve sisters went again to the ball, and *Michael* again followed them and crossed the lake in *Lina's* boat. This time it was the *Prince* who complained that the boat seemed very heavy.

"It is the heat," the *Princess* assured him. "I, too, have been feeling very warm."

During the ball she kept a sharp watch for the gardener's boy; but he was nowhere to be seen in the hall.

On the way back *Michael* plucked a branch from the wood with the gold-spangled leaves; and now it was the eldest *Princess* who heard the noise as it snapped.

"It is nothing," said *Lina;* "Only the hoot of the owl that roosts in the castle-turrets."

XI

When *Michael* handed her the bouquet next morning, she at once found the golden branch in it. So, staying a little behind her sisters as they went downstairs, she asked him in a low voice, "Where does this branch come from?"

"Your Royal Highness knows well enough," answered *Michael*.

"So you have followed us?"

"Yes, *Princess*."

"But how did you manage it? We never saw you."

"I hid myself," replied the Star-gazer quietly.

The *Princess* was silent for a moment. Then she said:

"You know our secret. Keep it!—and here is the reward of your discretion." She flung the boy a purse of gold.

"I do not sell my silence, *Princess*," answered *Michael*; and he walked away without picking up the purse.

XII

For three nights after this *Lina* neither saw nor heard anything extraordinary. On the fourth she heard a rustling among the diamond spangled leaves of the wood; and next morning there was a bediamonded branch in her bouquet.

She took the Star-gazer aside, and said to him in a harsh voice:

"You know what price my father has promised to pay for our secret?"

"I know, *Princess*," said *Michael.*

"Don't you mean to tell him?"

"That is not my intention."

"Why? Are you afraid?"

"No, *Princess*."

"What makes you so discreet, then?"

But *Michael* was silent.

XIII

Now *Lina's* sisters had seen her talking with the gardener's boy, and they twitted her about it.

"What prevents you marrying him?" asked the eldest. "Then you would become a gardener too, which, is a charming profession. You could live in a cottage at the end of the park, and help your husband to draw up water from the well, and to tie up our nosegays for us!"

At this the *Princess Lina* was very angry, and when the Star-gazer presented her bouquet she took it in a disdainful manner.

But he kept silence and continued to treat her respectfully. He never lifted his eyes to her; but all the day long, without seeing him, she felt him at her side.

At length one day she made up her mind and told her eldest sister what had happened.

"What!" cried the eldest *Princess*; "this rogue knows our secret, and you never told me! I must get rid of him without loss of time."

"But how?"

"Why, by having him taken to the dungeons, of course." For this was how, in old times, beautiful *Princesses* got rid of people who knew too much.

But you will be astonished to learn that the youngest sister did not seem at all to relish this method of stopping the mouth of the gardener's boy—who, after all, had said nothing to their father.

XIV

They agreed to submit the question to the other ten

sisters. All took the side of the eldest. "The rogue was dangerous," they agreed, "and should be locked up."

Thereupon the youngest sister stood up and declared that, if they laid a finger on the little garden-boy, she herself would go and tell their father the secret of the holes in their shoes!

So they had to find another way: and at last it was decided that *Michael* should be put to the test; that they would take him to the ball, and after supper they would give him to drink of a philtre—the same magic cup, in fact, by which all the *Princes* had been enchanted.

They sent for the Star-gazer, and asked him how he contrived to learn their secret. But this he would not tell.

Then, as agreed, the eldest sister spoke their command. He was to make ready and go with them that night.

He bowed and answered only:

"I will obey."

He had really been present, invisible, while they discussed what to do with him: and had heard all. But he had made up his mind to drink of the philtre and sacrifice himself to the happiness of his beloved.

Not wishing, however, to cut a poor figure at the ball

by the side of the other dancers, he hastened at once to the laurels, and said:

"My beautiful rose laurel, with the golden rake I have raked thee, with the golden watering pot I have watered thee, with the silken towel I have dried thee. Dress me like a Prince."

A beautiful pink flower blossomed on the laurel. *Michael* gathered it, and found himself in a moment clad in velvet, which was as black as the eyes of the little *Princess*, with a cap to match, a diamond aigrette, and a blossom of the rose laurel in his button-hole.

Thus attired he presented himself that evening before the *Duke of Bel-Œil*, and obtained leave to try and discover the secret. He looked so distinguished that no one would have suspected him for what he was—the gardener's boy.

XV

The twelve *Princesses* went upstairs to their bedchamber. *Michael* followed them and waited outside the door until they tapped on it as a signal that they were ready to start.

This time he did not cross in *Lina's* boat. He gave his arm to the eldest sister, and danced with each in turn—yes, and so gracefully that everyone was charmed with him. At last the time came for him to dance with the little *Princess*. She found him the best partner in the world; but he, for all his bliss, did not dare to speak a single word to her.

As he led her back to her place, she said to him in a slighting tone, "I congratulate you; for you must be at the summit of your wishes, being treated like a prince."

"Do not be afraid," said the Star-gazer gently; "You shall never be a gardener's wife."

The little *Princess* stared at him with a frightened face; but he left her without waiting for an answer.

When the satin slippers were worn through, the violins stopped and the negro boys set the table. *Michael* was seated next to the eldest sister, and opposite to the youngest. They gave him the most exquisite dishes to eat, and the most delicate wines to drink: and to turn his head the more completely, they loaded him with compliments and flattering speeches on every side.

But he took care not to be intoxicated either by the wine or by the compliments.

XVI

At last the eldest sister made a sign, and one of the black pages brought in a large golden goblet.

"The Enchanted Castle has no more secrets for you," she said to the Star-gazer, half ironically; "Let us drink to your triumph!"

He raised his eyes and rested them on the little *Princess* with one long, slow look: then quite steadily he lifted the cup.

"Don't drink!" cried out the little *Princess*, springing to her feet; "I would rather marry a gardener!"

With that she burst into tears.

But *Michael* flung the contents of the cup over his shoulder, vaulted across the table, and fell at *Lina's* feet. The rest of the *Princes* fell likewise at the knees of the *Princesses*, each of whom chose a husband and raised him to her side. The charm was broken.

The twelve couples embarked in the boats, which crossed back many times to fetch over the other *Princes*. Then in a troop they went back through the three woods, and had scarcely passed the door of the secret passage when a loud noise was heard from the distant shore of the lake, as the Enchanted Castle crumbled to earth in a heap.

They went straight to the room of the *Duke of Bel-Œil* who was just waking from sleep. *Michael* held in his hand the golden cup; and bending on one knee he revealed the secret of the holes in the shoes.

"Choose, then," said the *Duke*, "whichever you prefer."

"My choice is already made," answered the garden-boy, and he held out his hand to the youngest *Princess*, who blushed as she took it, lowering her eyes.

XVII

The *Princess Lina* did not become a gardener's wife. On the contrary, it was the gardener's boy, the Star-gazer, who became a *Prince*. But before the marriage ceremony the *Princess* insisted that her lover should tell her how he came to discover the secret.

So he showed her the two laurels which had helped him; and she, like a prudent girl, thinking they gave him too great an advantage over his wife, cut them off at the root and threw them into the fire.

And that is why the country girls go about singing :—

Nous n'irons plus au bois,
Les lauriers sont coupés,

and dancing in summer by the light of the moon.

ROSANIE

OR

THE INCONSTANT PRINCE

EVERYBODY knows that the Fairies, though as a rule they live for hundreds and hundreds of years, do sometimes die; because one day in every week they have to change into some animal or other, and then accidents are liable to happen. It was in this way that the *Queen of the Fairies* met her end. I cannot tell you the story here, but they gave her a magnificent funeral, and made speeches over her, and then (as the custom was), summoned a general Assembly to elect a new Queen.

There was a good deal of debating; but in the end everyone's choice lay between two, *Surcantine* and *Paridamie*, who in wit and talent were so equally matched that, intelligent though the Assembly was, it saw no way of preferring either without doing injustice to the other. In fairness, then, it was unanimously decided that whichever of the rivals could show the world the greater wonder should be the Queen. It was further resolved, before the Assembly broke up, that the wonder must be of a sort that appealed to persons of taste—no moving of mountains or manufacture of earthquakes or any such common fairy tricks, but something more refined altogether.

Following this instruction, *Surcantine* announced that she would undertake to produce a *Prince* whom nothing in the world could make constant; while *Paridamie* promised to display to mortal eyes a *Princess* whom no one could see and resist loving.

Finally the Assembly decided by vote that the two should be allowed to take their time: and to entrust the government of the Fairy Kingdom meanwhile to a

Commission of the four Senior Fairies, who were too old to have any ambitions of their own.

Now *Paridamie* had a long-standing friendship with a certain *King Bardondon*, a talented and accomplished Monarch, whose court was a model of all a court should be, alike in gallantry and in good behaviour. His Queen, *Balanice*, too, was a charming person. It is not often you see on the throne a husband and wife so delightful in their different ways yet so perfectly united.

They had but one child—a little daughter, whom they loved fondly: and because she had been born with a pretty rose printed in pink just below her white throat, they named her *Rosanie.* At four years of age she had already said things so astonishingly clever that some of the courtiers learnt them by heart and repeated them on all occasions.

But alas! in the middle of the night following the Fairies' Assembly, *Queen Balanice* started out of sleep with a piercing scream which not only woke the *King*, but fetched all the ladies of the bedchamber and all the guards and chamberlains running to her help.

"I have had a terrible dream!" she declared. "I dreamed that my little *Rosanie* had changed into a bouquet of roses; and while I held it, gazing at the flowers and caressing them, a pretty bird swooped down, snatched it from my hands and flew away with it . . . Run at once," she besought, "and see that nothing has happened to the *Princess!*"

They ran to her room. What was their dismay to find the small cot empty! They scattered in search all over the palace, the gardens, the grounds; they sought high and low; riders on horseback scoured the country for news: but all in vain. *Rosanie* had vanished. Not a trace of her could be found.

The *Queen* was inconsolable. The *King* too was stunned with sorrow: though as a man he hid something of his grief and, recovering strength of mind, applied himself to softening his dear wife's distress. Fearing for her health, he proposed to *Balanice* that they should retire and spend some days in a country-house they had built not far from the capital. *Balanice* readily consented, for grief and solitude are ever friends.

In the grounds of the country house was a lawn of turf enclosed by trees and shaped like a star, from the twelve points of which rayed out twelve straight green alleys. One day as they rested together here, sad and sorrowful, they looked up and saw along each of these alleys a peasant girl approaching. As the twelve damsels drew near, the *King* and *Queen* could not but remark how bright and healthful were their complexions, how modestly they bore themselves, and what honest country kindness shone in their faces: but—more remarkable yet—each carried, with particular care, a basket.

Still they advanced until, stepping forth on the lawn together and forming a ring, they laid their baskets at *Balanice's* feet.

"Most charming *Queen*," said they, curtseying—which is the proper way to address any Queen, though she be far less charming than was *Balanice*. How these country girls had learnt it you must guess for yourself—"Most charming *Queen*, accept what we bring to console your sorrow!"

With this they curtseyed again, withdrew quickly—each to her alley—and disappeared. *Balanice* eagerly opened the baskets . . . In each of the twelve she found a little baby-girl of about the same age as her own lost *Rosanie!*

At first sight of them her grief broke out afresh, and she wept bitterly. But by-and-by their pretty graces and infant ways so won upon her that she smiled through her tears. A moment later she was calling for nurses, nursemaids, wardrobe-maids, sending everywhere for dolls and toys by the cartload, and ordering sweets, cakes, chocolates by the basketful from all the best confectioners in the capital.

Strange to say, each of the twelve babes had, just beneath its throat, exquisitely printed on the white skin, a tiny pink rose.

The *Queen* was at once confronted by the difficulty of finding names for all of them. She had too much taste to christen them by inappropriate ones; and sufficient knowledge of the world to be aware that to choose appropriately for so many would be a long and tedious business. Had she not known ladies of the Court who would spend a fortnight at least before deciding how to name a lap-dog?

"*Rosanie*" was sacred to the child she had lost, and moreover, though most appropriate of all, was equally appropriate to all the twelve!

When you consider how unusual it is to have to christen twelve babies at once, I feel sure you will forgive *Queen Balanice* that she put the matter off for a while. In the meantime she gave orders that each should have a special colour assigned to it and be dressed in clothes of that colour: which was done, and when they were brought to the *Queen*, for her to play with them, she took the greatest delight in arranging them, so that they looked like a parterre of gay flowers around her.

But as they played and grew up, although all the twelve were fascinating, each developed a little character of her own, with some particular grace: and these little characters grew stronger with time, and these graces became so pronounced, that they gradually ceased to be known as "*Rose-red*," or "*Lily-white*," or "*Pearl-grey*," or "*Sky-blue*," or "*Primrose*," or "*Lavender*," or "*Apple-blossom*," or whatever their colour might be, and instead the *Queen*, still delaying to find ordinary names for them, would say:—

"Kiss me, *Beauty*," or "Come to me, my *Sweet*," or "A penny for your thoughts, my *Lady Pensive*," or "Dance my *Lady Gay*," or "Soft and fair, small *Lady Disdain*," or "Fie, my pretty *Coquette*," or (mockingly) "Your servant, *Madam Prue*!" and so on.

You can easily understand that, possessing these charms (each in its way, incomparable), the twelve princesses in time had no lack of suitors. The young gentlemen of the Court lost their hearts, all in turn, to one or the other, and princes were constantly arriving from foreign countries, attracted by report of their beauty and—yet more perhaps—by report of their aloofness. For these maidens, so different, yet so affectionate among themselves that each seemed necessary to all the others, had apparently no disposition to bestow their love elsewhere than on their adoptive parents, the *King* and *Queen*. They were gracious, indeed, to all who came in their way ; they even smiled on their suitors and tolerated them. But—it was strange : these loveliest creatures on earth continued all as discreet as they were lovely, and lived on with hearts untouched. Their affection, still turning inward upon one another, seemed proof against all attack from without.

* * * * *

It is time now that we turned to *Surcantine*. She, being pledged to find and educate a Prince who should be of all men the most fickle, fixed her hopes on a lad, son of a King who was cousin-german to *King Bardondon*. This lad—or, rather, this child (for he had but reached his eighth year)—this *Prince Miraflor*, to give him his right name—was her godson; and she had endowed him in his cradle with every grace of wit and of person. But she now attached herself to him and set to work to redouble, as he grew, whatever might attract the eyes of woman. She made him handsome beyond belief; she taught him address—how to give a witty turn to every word he uttered, and how, when uttering it, to use his eyes. She did not neglect, while making him an incomparable dancer, to instruct him in the manlier arts which women admire. He could shoot, ride, fence, swim—all as peerlessly as he dressed himself or made love. To his credit be it said that by nature he was brave as a lion, as by nature he had (if you will credit it) a heart as simple as gold. This indeed had been necessary to *Surcantine's* purpose, for without it she could never have bred up the look in his eyes, the tone of his voice, which went so straight to the hearts of others. Yet this, having been used to the full, was precisely what she had next to combat.

It was her capital difficulty; and most cleverly she contrived a way around it. She continued to inspire *Miraflor* with the noblest sentiments on every subject you can think upon, except upon women. Of women she

Felicia listens to the hen's story.

FELICIA

Page 62

The good Fairy commands the zephyrs to carry her son to the tower.

FELICIA

Page 62

The twelve sisters on their way to the dance.

THE TWELVE DANCING PRINCESSES

Page 82

When the cock crowed, the violins stopped.

THE TWELVE DANCING PRINCESSES

Page 84

She stopped as if to speak to him; then, altering her mind, went on her way.

THE TWELVE DANCING PRINCESSES

Page 86

"Don't drink!" cried out the little Princess, springing to her feet.

THE TWELVE DANCING PRINCESSES

Page 93

Queen Balanice has a terrible dream.

ROSANIE

Page 98

A look—a kiss—and he was gone.

ROSANIE

Page 105

carefully instilled into him the most careless contempt; teaching him that their hearts were only worth breaking because it became a Prince to break all he came across, as a matter of manly skill, like shooting game.

At the age of eighteen, then, *Miraflor* had made love to every lady in his father's Court and had tossed them all aside. The fairy *Surcantine* had taught him so well—his look and voice were so winning—that the ladies of the Court, each in her turn, scarcely dreamed of tying him to fidelity. His passing preference honoured them enough: and, after a few hearts had been broken, the rest were happy enough to boast of it. A look—a kiss—and he was gone. The worst was, on their part, that his preference became too capricious to boast about: and on his part, that conquests so easy became a bore.

He was, in fact, yawning over the difficulty of inventing a new attachment at home when an invitation arrived for him to visit the Court of his Great-uncle, *King Bardondon*.

He had heard, to be sure, of the wit and beauty to be found there, for these were celebrated throughout the world; and some word had reached him of the twelve Princesses whom no courtship could touch.

Here was a field for our conquering lover! He arrived, and was presented. It took him no time at all to determine that somewhere—by one of the twelve—his heart was engaged. No other Lady of *King Bardondon's* Court—beautiful as many were in comparison with the ladies whose hearts he had broken at home—could hold a candle to these.

The question was, whom to love first?—or, as he put it to himself, whom to love best?

He gazed upon *Beauty*, upon *Pensive*, upon *Gay*, upon *Prudence*, upon *Coquette*, upon *Faith*, *Caprice*, *Disdain*. Each was delicious in her different way: and, for the life of him, he could not make up his mind!

What heightened his embarrassment was that on their part each of them seemed to have forsaken her doubt and suspicion of men and to be gently inclined towards him as they had never before been towards any suitor. He was, indeed, nobody's suitor as yet, for between them he could not declare his choice. Yet all, without even beginning to quarrel, seemed to agree to meet him with a graciousness of her own.

Beauty smiled when he praised her eyes.

There was never so pretty a pout as *Disdain's*.

Gay kept him laughing.

Coquette intrigued him.

Sitting apart with *Pensive* he poured out his heart to her and felt that they had a common secret.

Sweet had a word to soothe all his woes.

Yet after all, *Prudence* would make the best housewife—if one wanted a wife for wear. He was not sure that he did, or that he did not.

Well this would have been a sad predicament for most lovers, but *Prince Miraflor* had been thoroughly trained. When he saw them apart he wooed each one separately; when he saw them together he adored them all! The Fairy *Surcantine* was radiant over her success. Twelve sweethearts at once! Was ever such a miracle of inconstancy? She proclaimed it as one sure of her triumph. *Paridamie* said never a word.

Prince Miraflor's father wrote urging him—nay, commanding him—to return; but in vain. In vain, too, did he write that he had found a bride for his son, an excellent match, close at home. *Miraflor* was deaf to proposals, entreaties, commands. Nothing in the world could tear him from his heart's twelve sole and sovereign mistresses!

One day *Queen Balanice* gave a fine garden-party. All the Court was there, and there as usual was *Prince Miraflor* flitting like a butterfly from one to another of the twelve Princesses, enchanted by each in turn. Suddenly the hum of conversation ceased at the sound of a louder and yet louder humming in the sky. The guests looked up in alarm, which increased as they saw a small army of bees approaching at a great speed and each bee growing larger and larger until their bodies darkened the sun. The ladies screamed and ran wildly in every direction, fearing to be stung. *Prince Miraflor*, who knew not which of his charmers to follow and protect, was left standing alone; when to his horror, and the horror of all, twelve of the largest bees detached themselves from the main body, descended, and pouncing each upon one of the *Princesses* caught her aloft into the air. A thousand outcries answered the poor maidens as they shrieked for help; but what could be done? The crowd stared helplessly and *Prince Miraflor* ran hither and thither as the swarm wheeled and winged its way off until lost in the blue sky.

This amazing occurrence plunged the whole Court into deepest mourning. As for *Miraflor*, after an access of despair so wild that everyone feared for his reason, he fell into an excessive dejection that made everyone fear for his life. To all consolation he turned a deaf ear. For other people find affliction enough in the loss of a dearest one, whereas he had lost twelve!

The *Fairy Surcantine* sped in all diligence to see what could be done for her pet Prince. She brought him romances full of the misfortunes of lovers, but he would not open them; he turned on his heel when she offered him portraits of beautiful women to add to his extensive collection in which he had formerly taken so much pride. In short, all joy in her triumph was dashed; for she saw *Miraflor* wasting away and could do nothing to save him.

One day, as he wandered alone, a prey to unavailing regrets, he heard of a sudden, from every side of the royal gardens, loud exclamations of surprise, joy, admiration. For his part he felt no curiosity to learn what was happening: he had lost all interest in life.

And yet, had he looked up, he would have been well rewarded. For what had attracted everyone's attention was the spectacle of an enormous crystal chariot slowly approaching through the air on which its wheels seemed to glide while its transparent sides glittered in the sunshine with a million darting rays. Three pairs of lovely damsels drew the car, their wings beating in time, to a soft rhythm: while a taller maiden guided the six-in-hand with reins of rose-coloured ribbon. Behind this charioteer, on the floor of the car, stood a bevy of damsels whose wings too waved and sparkled as, gathered in a ring, they held up their festoons and garlands of roses to form a canopy over the *Fairy Paridamie*, and, by her side, a Princess whose loveliness out-dazzled even the car and its moving equipage.

The chariot, after hovering a moment or two, sank and touched earth at the foot of the palace steps. *Paridamie* alighted and extending her hand to the lovely Stranger led her up and indoors to the *Queen's* apartments. They had indeed some trouble to make their way, such a crowd of Courtiers were pressing around, forgetting all manners in their eagerness to gaze on such surpassing beauty. The guards, taken by surprise and not a little flurried, had much ado to clear a passage, and even when the visitors reached the royal presence, loud murmurs of admiration filled the corridors behind, where excitement had for the moment broken down all Court etiquette.

"Great *Queen*," said the *Fairy Paridamie*, "behold

your daughter *Rosanie!* This is she whom—to your sorrow, but for her good—I stole from you."

After the *Queen* had embraced her long-lost *Rosanie*, and was a little recovered from her first transports of joy, she turned to *Paridamie*.

"But my twelve lost daughters!—though I have recovered this dearest one, shall I never see them again?"

The good *Paridamie* avoided a direct answer.

"Dear Madam," said she very gently, sinking her voice, "if you can trust me, before long you will have ceased to miss them,"—and, as if to escape further questions she hurried away to her chariot, which, as she set foot in it, vanished quick as lightning.

News of this wonder speedily reached *Prince Miraflor*. But though it was difficult to tell whether the messengers panted from admiration or from exhaustion, all their reports concerning *Rosanie*, her marvellous return and her even more marvellous beauty, made little impression on his mind. He heard, but with impatience, and it was with some difficulty they persuaded him to go and pay his respects to his fair cousin. Indeed in the end he yielded out of mere politeness, having reminded himself that he was, after all, a guest of *King Bardondon*.

At first sight of the *Princess Rosanie* he started and flushed. It was with a sort of anger against himself that after such a loss as he had sustained he should still be capable of recognising any beauty in the world. And truly *Rosanie's* beauty alone would never have availed to divorce his thoughts from those he mourned, had it not been that in five minutes talk with him she let peep out, one by one, hint by hint, all the gifts, charms, graces,—all the gentle traits of character—nay, even all the pretty tricks of voice and gesture, he had been wont to adore in this, that, or the other of the twelve Princesses.

After all there is a great deal to be said for making love to one person at a time!

When you have arrived at that, the rest is easy: though it was yet somewhat bewildering to *Prince Miraflor* to find himself, ten minutes later, entreating his fair cousin to marry him. Most bewildering of all was the certainty, in his mind, that he meant every word he was saying!

I think that somehow or other, the *Princess Rosanie* must have detected his sincerity. At any rate she looked him in the eyes for quite a long time, and then she said "Yes."

No sooner had the word passed her lips than above

them, to a flourish of trumpets, *Paridamie* appeared, seated in a magnificent chariot. It was indeed the chariot of the *Queen of Fairies:* for word of the triumph had been carried in a flash, and the kingdom was hers by right, now and henceforth.

She alighted and told the story of her success; how she had carried off little *Rosanie*, and how, dividing her character into twelve parts, she had separately brought each to perfection, that each might separately enchant *Prince Miraflor* and, when, at last united, cure him of inconstancy once and for ever.

It is pleasant to be able to add that *Fairy Surcantine* handsomely admitted herself beaten, and—whether of her own generosity, or because the charms of *Rosanie* vanquished her heart as it had vanquished her plans—sent the most beautiful of wedding presents.

The marriage was an entire success. *Rosanie* loved *Miraflor* as much as had all the twelve Princesses put together, and *Miraflor* was constant to *Rosanie* all the rest of their lives, which were extraordinarily long and happy.

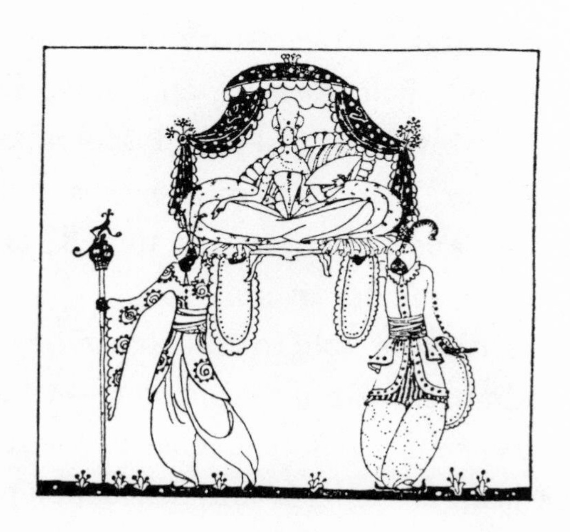

THE MAN WHO NEVER LAUGHED

ONCE upon a time there lived at Highgate, to the north of London, a man possessed of great wealth which he had amassed by the sale of tea in the City. He had servants and horses and carriages; pictures by the most eminent contemporary artists, musical-boxes, hot-houses in which he grew peaches for exhibition, a fine lawn with an araucaria-tree in the midst of it; in short everything that could bring content to one who practised moderation and observed regular habits.

In process of time he departed from this world, bequeathing his estate to an only son for whom he had procured a commission in the Grenadier Guards. This youth was tractable, indeed, by nature, and desirous to please; but averse to steady exertion. Scarcely had he come into his inheritance before he removed to a fine mansion in Piccadilly; abandoning a military career, addicted himself to eating and drinking and to the hearing of instruments of music; frequented the theatres (and these not of the best); delighted in the postures of dancing girls; was ready at any time to wager on the speed of race-horses; and set up a tilbury, in which he daily drove himself about the Park, by the barracks where his former comrades-in-arms were still patiently occupied in drilling. Amid these distractions he forgot that there must be an end even to such a sum as two hundred thousand pounds, until one day he awoke to find that his riches had taken wing, to the last penny.

Thereupon, recognising the mutability of all human affairs, he sold his house in Piccadilly with the rest of his possessions, down to the tilbury—the purchaser of which allowed him to sit for hire on the back seat in a liveried suit, so that he still was driven about the Park, and saw the fashionable world, albeit at a different angle.

Even thus it might have gone well with him. But old habits are not soon unlearnt; those connected with the pleasures of the table last of all, perhaps. His master having occasion to reprove him for a too loose adherence to the back seat of the tilbury, and one word leading to another (as it so often does), our *Young Man* found himself dismissed.

He now set up in business as a Screever, or pavement-artist, on the Thames Embankment, where, seating himself upon the flag-stones in a place of much traffic, he reproduced in coloured chalks, for the amusement of the passing throng, such salient features as memory preserved of his father's collection of masterpieces.

In this employ he continued for two years, until one day as he sat beside a drawing of Still Life deploring to himself the small encouragement given to the graphic arts in this country, he was accosted by an old gentleman of benevolent aspect, but sorrowful, who indicated an object in the picture with the point of his walking-stick, and said:

" A banana! "

" Venerable stranger," said the *Artist*, " you have discerned aright. It is a banana. Avoid therefore to tread on it."

" It is plain to me," said the *Stranger*, " that you were either born for some other pursuit than that which you now follow, or perchance have stepped down from a higher destiny."

" O *Uncle!* " cried the *Young Man*, " Did you know me, then, in the days of my prosperity? "

" I am not aware," answered the *Stranger*, " that I ever set eyes on you in my life. But in your polite address I read traces of former affluence, while your notion of a banana suggests that you were late in making the acquaintance of that cheap but nutritious fruit."

" O *Uncle*," said the *Young Man*, improving on this hint, " I am indeed what destiny has made me. But hast thou, O affable one, any light employment to offer with a sufficient salary? Then, indeed, we shall be coming to business."

To this the *Stranger* replied: " O sagacious youth, even so; I desire to employ and to reward thee. There dwell with me in one house ten retired *Stockbrokers*, myself being the eleventh, and we have no one to go to market for us, or to keep our accounts. Thou shalt receive from us food and clothing, with benefits in money and perquisites. It may be also that Heaven will restore thee to affluence by our means."

"O *Uncle!*" said the *Young Man*, "of a surety thou must have dropped from the skies!"

"Stay!" interposed the *Stockbroker*, checking his alacrity. "There is a condition to be observed. It is that thou observe silence with respect to the things thou shalt see us do: and in particular that, when thou seest us weep, thou shalt not ask the reason of our weeping."

"And is that all?" asked the *Young Man*. "Right-O!"

II

So the *Young Man* abandoned his drawing of bananas and what-not and followed the *Stockbroker*, who led him first to a Turkish Bath, where he was stripped and cleansed of the pollutions of poverty. Further, perceiving that the *Young Man's* body was comely and in no way deformed, the *Stockbroker* sent to an outfitter's for ready-made raiment and body linen. He sent also to demand the attendance of a fashionable barber. Finally this good man, when the youth was bathed, shaven, scented and apparelled, hailed a cab and instructed the driver to convey them first across the river, then in a westerly direction, until they reached the environs of Richmond.

Our *Young Man* had not ceased to congratulate himself on this happy reversal of fortune, when his protector called the cab to a halt beside a wall of unusual height and blank save for a low doorway. They alighted, dismissed the cabman with a fee, and entered the demesne. The high wall enclosed a garden, parcelled out into beds of geometrical patterns and ablaze with pelargoniums, petunias and calceolarias commingled in the worst possible taste. In the midst of this pleasance stood a mansion shaped like a game-pie, with moulded ornaments in stucco and windows protected by Venetian blinds. The *Stockbroker* opened the door with a latchkey and led the way through the hall into a large saloon in which sat ten elderly men mournfully attired, arranged on chairs around the wall, facing one another and weeping. The *Young Man* had a mind to ask why they thus comported themselves, but forbore, remembering the condition imposed.

From the saloon his friend led him to an office and showed him a chest or strong box standing in the corner.

"My son," said he, "this chest contains thirty thousand pieces of gold. Also in the drawer of the writing table yonder thou will find a book full of blank cheques. Employ these riches at thy discretion; expend them upon us and thyself, observing what is just to either and remembering that, for all our melancholy, we like to dine comfortably, without ostentation, in the middle of the day."

"Right-O!" said the *Young Man*, and therewith became the steward of the *Eleven Stockbrokers*, upon whose need he expended the monies entrusted to him, giving satisfaction and keeping strict account of all payments.

In the course of the second year one of the *Stockbrokers* died and was cremated. The surviving ten consigned his ashes to a bed in the back garden. So death took these *Stockbrokers* one by one, until at length there remained only the one who had hired our *Young Man* to their service.

III

These two, then, remained in that mansion for one year and five months, at the expiry of which time the aged *Stockbroker* fell sick—so sick, indeed, that the *Young Man* (for so we shall call him, albeit he had now reached the age of thirty-five) fell into despair of his life, and thus addressed him:

"O *Uncle*, I have served you, nor failed in my service, for these twelve years, according to my industry and ability."

"Yea, O my son," said the dying *Stockbroker*, "thou sayest no more than the truth. Surely thou hast served me well and these others that have been taken."

Then said the *Young Man*, "O my master, thou liest in a parlous state, and it cannot be denied."

"It cannot be denied. What follows?"

"I greatly desire," said the *Young Man*, "to hear of thee, master, what hath been the cause why thou and those others evermore wept and continued to weep, though I have used the moneys to tempt your appetites with good things."

"If I tell the cause, O my son, it will but tempt

thee to follow the path of our affliction."

"Nevertheless," said the *Young Man*, "I desire to hear."

The *Stockbroker* sighed deeply. "In the room below this is a door which for these many years has not been open. The key used to hang with my other keys upon the ring which will soon become yours."

"Alas, my *Father!*" lamented the *Young Man*.

"But I have cast it away where no man can find it. If, then, thou desire to avoid the affliction into which, one by one, we fell, open not that door. But if thou desire that what befell us should also befall thee, then open it, and thou shalt learn the cause of our long weeping: but thou wilt repent, and repentance will come to late to avail thee."

Then the *Stockbroker's* sickness increased upon him, and he died; and the *Young Man* washed the body with his own hands and shrouded it, and burned it according to his instructions, and laid the ashes beside the other ashes in the garden.

IV

He then took possession of the house and dwelt in

it, having riches enough and to spare; notwithstanding which he could not rest, for his mind dwelt continually upon the conduct of the eleven *Stockbrokers*.

One day while he sat pensive, pondering the last words of his benefactor and wondering why he was on no account to open the door, the thought occurred to him that he might at least have a look at it, for he did not remember any such door in the house.

So he sought the apartment beneath that in which the old *Stockbroker* had died, and after a while he found the door, behind a hanging of draperies. The spiders had woven their webs about it, and upon it were four massy locks of steel. When the *Young Man* beheld it he remembered how solemn had been the caution laid upon him, and dropping the curtain, he fled from the room. Yet his soul longed to open the door, and kept whispering to him. For the space of seven days he resisted it, but on the eighth day his soul overcame him, and he said, "I must open the door, and see what will happen to me in consequence. To-morrow morning I will do it." Upon this resolve he retired to bed.

That same night, as it happened, a *Thief* broke into the house; for he had been attracted by the report of the *Young Man's* great possessions. The *Young Man*—who slept lightly by reason of his meditation—awoke to the sound of the man's entry, and going downstairs, caught him in the act of prising open a safe which contained much gold and had been extensively advertised as burglar-proof.

Then the *Thief* (who was not muscular) would have fled; but the *Young Man* detained him, using mild words.

"Friend," said he, "I have seen it written that Exchange is no Robbery. Accept, then, this silver cup, and for payment leave me those instruments of your trade—of which, if I may say so, you seem to have a serviceable collection."

The *Thief* was only too glad to escape on these terms, and freely expressed his approval of them.

"Go in peace," said the *Young Man*, and was left with the tools. It now appeared evident to him that destiny as well as inclination commanded him to open the door.

Accordingly he arose early and did so, after he had broken the locks.

V

The door opened upon a passage, very narrow and dark, along which he walked for the space of three hours, and lo! he came forth into daylight upon the bank of an exceeding broad river, and upon a quay, by the side of which a boat lay moored.

The *Young Man* stepped into the boat, took the oars and cast off, deciding to row with the current. But indeed he could not have pulled against it, so irresistibly the great river flowed. It cost him all his strength, when out in full stream, to keep steerage way on the boat and her head pointing straight. Before he knew it, the river had swept him out to sea and upon the beach of an island, where, the boat being broken upon a submerged rock, he waded ashore, giving thanks to Heaven for his escape.

The island appeared to have no inhabitants; but its trees bore an abundance of fruit, and he had little difficulty in sustaining life. He felt a conviction that his destiny had not cast him upon this deserted spot to end his days here, but rather as a pause and a preparation for some new adventure. Wherefore he spent the most of his time on the beach with his eyes fixed on the sea.

And in this he was right; for on the third day as he sat thus, the sail of a vessel appeared upon the sea, like a star in the sky. He gazed and gazed as the vessel drew nearer, and soon he perceived her to be a ship of war; but of what nation he could not guess, for the ensign she flew bore a red rose on a white ground.

The ship cast anchor at some distance from the island, and lowered a boat. Thereupon the *Young Man* did indeed rub his eyes, for the eight rowers were eight damsels, and a ninth damsel steered. They brought the boat to shore on the beach above which he sat, and there they disembarked; nor had he but barely time to mark that they were of exceeding beauty, when they approached him, and the damsel who had been steers-woman took his hand and kissed it, saying:

"Thou art the *King*, the bridegroom!"

The *Young Man* offering no objection to this, they led him to the boat and rowed him off to the ship; and still as he drew near to her and came alongside and climbed on deck, he was the more puzzled to guess to what Navy she belonged. For her guns were of gold, and around the muzzle of each, at its port-hole, hung a garland of flowers; the decks were spread with carpets; the sails were of silk and the ropes of twisted silk; the tops swarmed with singing-birds; while the capstan was a maypole, around which a score of the crew started to dance as they weighed anchor.

Then the *Young Man*, being conducted to the poop, reposed himself on cushions, while to the sound of guitars and mandolines the ship headed about and sped over the depths of the sea. Twilight fell, then night—the one violet coloured, the other velvet-purple, as though the sky were a bed of pansies with the stars for eyes. A supper was brought to him, with fruits and rare wines and sherbets, whereof he ate and drank, the while he discussed the remarkable beauty of the weather with the helmswoman, encouraged by a footnote on the menu—"*You are invited to talk with the Damsel at the Wheel. She has been selected for her Gifts of Conversation.*"

But he asked not to whom the ship belonged, nor whither he was being carried. For he felt sure this adventure was all a dream, and that he would awake again on the beach of the Island.

So, having smoked two excellent cigars and begged

everyone's pardon for his drowsiness, he fell asleep indeed.

VI

Awaking at daybreak, he found himself still on ship board: and the ship was drawing near to a fair land, with a range of snowy mountains for sky-line, and forests at their base, and green pastures stretching down from the foot of the forests to the shore, on which was gathered a vast army awaiting the ship's approach.

Again the anchor was dropped and a boat lowered to carry him ashore, where on landing he was amazed not only by the numbers of the soldiery, but by their comeliness also and their brilliant apparel. They led forward five young horses, their saddles and trappings studded with all manner of precious stones. The *Young Man* chose the one most to his mind and mounted; the others were assigned to four standard-bearers, of whom two rode before him and two behind. The troops disposed themselves in two divisions, to right and left. Trumpets sounded, drums and cymbals were beaten, and the immense procession started to march inland.

Still as he rode amid the music and the waving of banners, with those many thousands of feet marching in rhythm behind him, the *Young Man* moved forward as though in a dream; until the host came to a verdant meadow of many acres in extent, begirt with trees, and by streams parcelled into green lawns beside which stood a number of pavilions. From this meadow the slope of the land rose, through a wilderness of gardens full of flowers and singing birds, to a palace fair beyond imagination. As the *Young Man* reined up his horse in wonder, lo! a second army even larger than that which escorted him came pouring down from the palace and overflowed the terraces and filled all the wide meadow: and in the midst of this army rode a *King* heavily veiled and all alone, but with a company of foot-guards in rank on either side.

The *King* alighted to greet his guest. The *Young Man* alighted also, and they met with the most courteous salutation.

"More than any in the world thou art welcome to us," said the *King*; and, remounting, they rode side by side, up the hill to the palace.

There, by the palace steps, the *King* took the *Young*

Man by the hand and led him up to a great hall, where were two thrones of gold. And when the *Young Man* had been conducted to the greater throne of honour, the *King* seated himself on the other and withdrew the veil from his face, and behold! it was no King at all but a maiden more beautiful than the day, a lady of elegance and extreme loveliness, of conceit and amorous dis-simulation.

"Know, O welcome guest," said she, "that I am *Queen* of this realm, and all these troops, whether of cavalry or of infantry, are women even as I. There are not among them any men. The men in this land till and sow and reap; they thresh and garner; they also build and conduct all our commerce. Our governors and our magistrates, and our warriors on sea and on land are women every one. But thou art my bridegroom, and the lord of us all."

Then the *Young Man* would have knelt to her (so beautiful was she) and would have kissed the step of her throne: but she forbade him, saying—

"Art thou content to have me for wife?"

"O *Queen*," said he—"O *Queen* and mistress, I am less than the least of thy servants!"

But "Nay," she replied; "thou art lord of me and of us all henceforth. All this kingdom is thine save what lies beyond that little door"—and here she pointed to one. "All other doors thou mayst open, as thou hast opened the heart of thy handmaid: but not this one, or repentance will come when it is to late to avail thee."

With this she clapped her hands and there entered a number of staid grey-haired women, her councillors, bringing with them a male lawyer, behind whom followed a crowd of witnesses to attest the marriage contract.

So the *Young Man* was married to the most beautiful of creatures, and led forth his bride; and the two armies in the meadow lifted up their voices and cheered together.

VII

In this fashion, then, the *Young Man* achieved a wife and a kingdom, and for the space of seven years lacked nothing of felicity.

But one day his eyes fell on the door which his well-beloved had forbidden him to open, and he began to reason with himself, saying, "As it was with that other door, why should it not be with this? Lo! by disregarding the counsel of the old *Stockbroker* I have spent these seven years in abundant happiness. It may well be therefore that this door conceals a yet ampler destiny, and that through it I may pass unto treasures exceeding those which I now enjoy."

Thus reasoning he broke the lock and opened the door.

Then, as before, the *Young Man* found himself in a dim passage, along which he groped (as it seemed) for three hours when he was aware of a figure standing some way ahead in his path. Drawing nearer he perceived the figure to be that of an old man, dishevelled, with dust on his hair, of woe-begone aspect: and, as he yet approached, the figure opened its lips and said:

"No welcome to a face that will never be happy!"

Then the *Young Man* stretched forth both hands, entreating to pass: but they groped upon the smooth face of a mirror.

"Out of my way!" he cried. "There is a foul trick in this mirror—as, dotard, thou canst be no reflection of me, who am yet young and comely!"

Thereupon, as he dashed out both hands to strike the old man and hurl him aside, the mirror broke into ten thousand pieces, and he passed through it.

And lo! he stood in the room of his villa at Richmond, whence he had first set forth: only there was now no doorway in the wall, and the mirror over the mantelpiece told him that his were indeed the withered face and form he had encountered in the passage.

Therefore this *Young Man*, who now was *Old*, sat himself down upon a couch in the empty room, and gazing upon the horsehair covered furniture, and the prints which hung around the walls, he reflected upon what he had seen of affluence and glory and honour, and the parading of troops before him, and of commanding and forbidding: and thereat he wept and fell into a deep dejection. But yet he hoped somewhat that it might be granted to him to return and see again his wife and that kingdom.

But while he sat lamenting, a voice called in his ear:

"How great and many were the delights! Even so many and so heavy must be the sighs!"

Hearing this, the *Young Man*—who indeed was *Old*—knew of a surety that for him there could be no return, and understood why those men, now dead, had sat around and wept out what remained of their lives.

Whereupon he excused them, and going up unto his own chamber, fasted and prayed, relinquishing all wine and food and pleasant scents and laughter, until he died.

So the rate collector came in time to that house for the rates, and found none. But they buried the body by the side of the *Eleven Stockbrokers*.

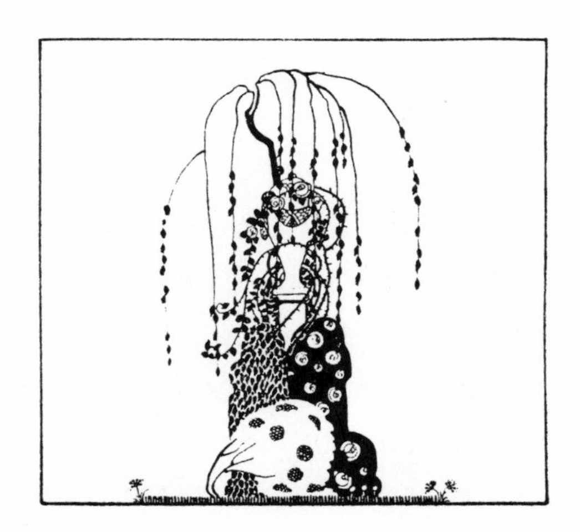

JOHN AND THE GHOSTS

IN the kingdom of *Illyria* there lived, not long ago, a poor woodcutter with three sons, who in time went forth to seek their fortunes. At the end of three years they returned by agreement, to compare their progress in the world. The eldest had become a lawyer, the second a merchant; and each of these had won riches and friends. But *John*, the youngest, who had enlisted in the army, could only show a cork leg and a medal.

"You have made a sad business of it," said his brothers; "Your medal is worthless except to a collector

Each was delicious in her different way, and he could not make up his mind!

ROSANIE

Page 106

The Young Man did not ask to whom the ship belonged or whither he was being carried.

THE MAN WHO NEVER LAUGHED

Page 128

"Out of my way!" he cried. "There is a foul trick in this mirror."

THE MAN WHO NEVER LAUGHED

Page 133

The Princess of Illyria had not smiled for a whole year.

JOHN AND THE GHOSTS

Page 139

"Your soul!"—"My soul!" they kept saying, according to whether they won or lost.

JOHN AND THE GHOSTS

Page 141

Prince Bismarck discovers the soldier.

THE CZARINA'S VIOLET

Page 153

The old woman knew why the soldier stood on the grass plot.

THE CZARINA'S VIOLET

Page 161

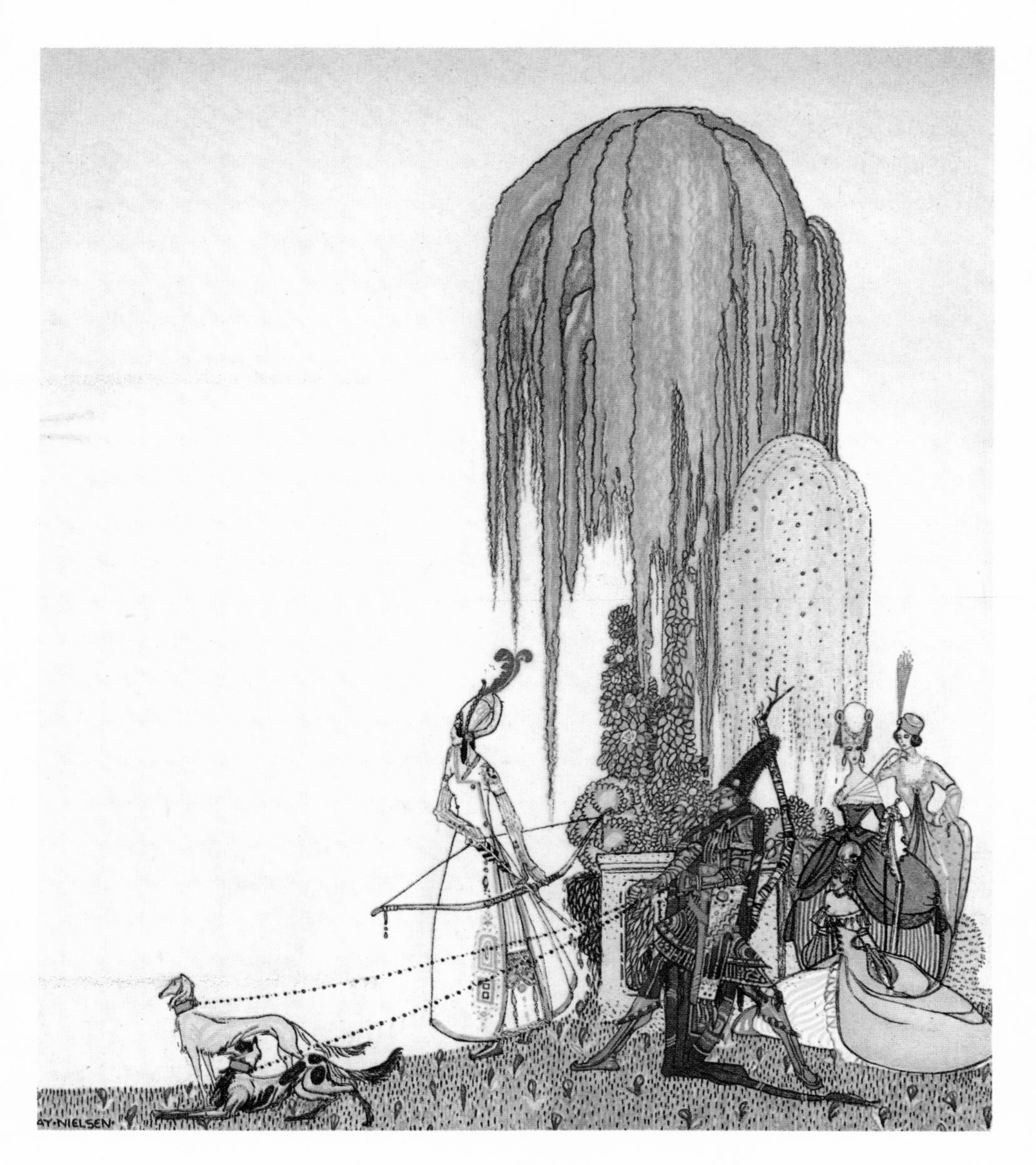

The ladies of the court were famous archers when the Czarina was a bride.

THE CZARINA'S VIOLET

Page 161

of such things, and your leg a positive disadvantage. Fortunately we have influence; and since you are our brother, we must see what we can do for you."

Now the *King of Illyria* lived at that time in his capital, in a brick palace at the end of a great park. He kept the park open to all, and allowed no one to build in it. But the richer citizens, who were so fond of their ruler that they could not live out of his sight, had their houses just beyond the Park, in the rear of the Palace, on a piece of ground which they called Palace Gardens. The name was a little misleading, for the true gardens lay in front of the Palace, where children of all classes played among the trees and flower-beds and artificial ponds. The *King* often sat there and watched them, because he took delight in children, and because the sight of them cheered his only daughter, who had fallen into a deep melancholy. But the rich citizens clung to the name, for it gave a pleasant neighbourly air to their roadway, and showed what friendliness there was between the monarch of Illyria and his people.

At either end you entered the roadway (if you were allowed) by an iron gate, and each gate had a sentry-box beside it, and a tall beadle, and a notice-board to save him the trouble of explanation. The notice ran :—

> *PRIVATE. The Beadle has orders to refuse admittance to all Waggons, Tradesmen's Carts, Hackney Coaches, Donkeys, Beggars, Disorderly Characters, or Persons carrying Burdens.*

A sedentary life had told so severely upon one of the two beadles that he could no longer squeeze into his box with dignity or read his newspaper there with any comfort. He resigned, and *John* obtained the appointment by his brothers' interest, in spite of his cork leg.

He had now a bright blue suit with scarlet pipings, a fashionable address, and very little to do. But the army had taught him to be active, and for lack of better exercise he took to thinking. This came near to bring him into trouble. One evening he looked out of his sentry-box and saw a mild, somewhat sad-featured old gentleman approaching the gate.

"No admittance," said *John*.

"Tut tut!" said the old gentleman. "I'm the King."

John looked at the face on his medal. Sure enough there was a resemblance. "But all the same," said he, pointing to the notice board, "Your Majesty carries a burden, and the folks along this road are mighty particular."

The *King* sighed heavily.

"It's about the *Princess*, my daughter," said he. "She has not smiled for a whole year."

"I'll warrant I'd make her," said *John*.

"I'll warrant you could not," said the *King*. "She will never smile again until she is married."

"Then," replied *John*, "speaking with all respect, why don't you marry her up and have done with it?"

The *King* shook his head.

"There's a condition attached," said he. "Maybe you have heard of the famous Haunted House in Berkeley Square? Well, the condition is that every suitor for my daughter's hand must spend a night alone in that house; and if he survive and be ready to persevere with his wooing, he must return a year later with his bride and spend the night of his marriage there."

"And very handy," said *John*; "for there's a wedding cake shop at the corner."

The *King* sighed again.

"Unhappily, none survive. One hundred and fifty-seven have essayed the adventure, and not a man of them but has either lost his wits or run for it."

"Well," said *John*, breathing on his medal and polishing it with his cuff, "I've been afraid of numbers of men in my time—"

"That's a poor confession for a soldier," put in the *King*.

"—when they all happened to come at me together. But I've never yet met the ghost that could frighten me; and if Your Majesty will give me the latch-key, I'll try my fortune this very night."

It could not be done in this free-and-easy way; but at eight o'clock, after *John* had visited the Palace and taken an oath in the *Princess's* presence (which was his first sight of her), he was driven down to the house beside the *Lord Chamberlain*, who admitted him to the dark front hall and hastily slamming the door upon him, scuttled back as quickly as possible into his brougham.

John struck a match, and as he did so he heard the carriage roll away. The walls were bare of pictures, and the floor and great staircase ahead of him carpetless.

As the match flickered out he caught a glimpse of a pair of feet moving up the stairs: that was all—only feet.

"I'll catch up with the calves on the landing, maybe," said he. Striking another match, he followed them up.

The feet turned aside on the landing and led him into a room on the right. He paused on the threshold, drew a candle from his pocket, lit it, and stared about him. The room was of vast size, bare and dusty, with crimson hangings, gilt panels, and one huge chandelier of cut glass, from which, as from the ceiling and cornices, long cobwebs trailed down like creeping plants. Beneath the chandelier a dark shadow ran along the boards. The feet crossed it towards the fireplace; and as they did so, *John* saw them smeared with blood. They reached the fireplace and vanished.

Scarcely had this happened before the end of the room began to glow with an unearthly light. *John*, whose poverty had taught him to be economical, promptly blew out his candle. A moment later two men entered, bearing a coffin between them. They rested it upon the floor, seated themselves upon it, and began to cast dice. "Your soul!"—"My soul!" they kept saying in hollow tones, according as they won or lost. At length one of them—a tall man in a cavalier's wig, with a face extraordinarily pale—flung a hand to his brow, rose, and staggered from the room. The other sat scowling and anon twisting his black moustache with an evil smile. He wore a patch over one eye, and *John* (who by this time had found a seat in a far corner) thought him the most poisonous-looking villain he had ever seen: but as the minutes passed and nothing happened, he turned his back to the light and pulled out a penny novel. His literary taste was shocking, and when it came to romance he liked the incidents to follow one another with extreme rapidity.

He was interrupted by a blood-curdling groan, and the first ruffian broke into the room, dragging by its grey locks the body of an old man. A young girl followed, weeping and protesting, with dishevelled hair, and behind her came a priest who carried a brazier full of glowing charcoal. The maiden cast herself forward on the corpse, but the two scoundrels dragged her from it by force. "The money!" demanded the dark one. She drew from her bosom a small key and cast it at his feet. "My per-romise!" hissed the other between his teeth. "Quick, Reverend Father! Over this coffin—man and wife!" She wrenched her hand away, and thrust him backward, as the priest stepped forward with a red-hot iron he had drawn from the brazier.

John thought it about time to interfere.

"I beg your pardon," said he, stepping forward: "but

I suppose you really *are* ghosts?"

"We are unhallowed spirits," answered the dark one impressively, "who return to blight the living with the spectacle of our awful crimes."

"Meaning me?" asked *John*.

"Ay, rash youth! and to destroy you to-night if you contract not, upon your soul, to return with your bride and meet us here a twelve month hence."

"H'm!" said *John* to himself; "they are three to one, and after all, that is precisely what I came for. I suppose," he added aloud, "some form of contract is usual in business of this kind?"

The dark man drew out pen and parchment.

"Hold forth your hand," he commanded. As *John* held it out affably, thinking he meant to shake it over the bargain, the fellow drove the pen into his wrist until the blood spurted.

"Now sign!"

"Sign!" echoed the other villain.

"Sign!" echoed the lady.

"Oh, very well, miss. If you are in this swindle, too, my mind is easier," said *John*, and signed his name with a flourish. "But a bargain is a bargian, gentlemen; and what security have I for your part in it?"

"Our sign manual!" answered the priest terribly, and the same moment pressing his branding-iron hard upon *John's* ankle.

A smell of burnt cork arose as *John* stooped to clap his hand over the scorched stocking. When he looked up again his visitors had vanished; and a moment later the unearthly light, too, died away.

But the coffin remained for evidence that *John* had not been dreaming. He re-lit his candle and examined it. "Just the thing for me," he exclaimed, finding it to be a mere shell of pine boards, loosely nailed together, and painted black. "I was beginning to shiver."

He knocked the coffin to pieces, crammed them into the fireplace, and very soon had a grand fire blazing, before which he sat and finished his penny novel, and so dropped off into a sound sleep.

The *Lord Chamberlain* arrived early next morning and, finding him stretched there, at first broke into lamentations over the fate of yet another personable young man. He changed his tune, however, when *John* sat up, rubbed his eyes, and demanded to be told the time.

"But are you really alive? We must drive back at

once and tell His Majesty."

"Stay a moment," said *John*. "There is a brother of mine, a lawyer in the City. He will be arriving at his office about this time, and you must drive me there; for I have a document here of a sort, and must have it stamped, to be on the safe side."

So into the City he was driven beside the *Lord Chamberlain*, and there had his leg stamped and filed for reference; and, having purchased another, was conveyed back to the Palace, where the King received him with open arms.

He was now a favoured guest at Court, and had frequent opportunities of seeing and conversing with the *Princess*, with whom he soon fell deeply in love. But as the months passed and the time drew near for their marriage, he grew silent and thoughtful; for he feared to expose her, even in his company, to the sights he had witnessed in the Haunted House.

He thought and thought . . . One fine afternoon he snapped his fingers suddenly, ordered a carriage, and drove into the City again—this time to the office of his second brother, the merchant.

"I want," said he, "a loan of a thousand pounds."

The brother made no difficulty about this, knowing *John's* prospects and his influence at court; but advanced the money and warmly shook hands with him over his approaching nuptials.

They were celebrated with great pomp; and in the evening the *King*, who had been shedding tears at intervals throughout the ceremonies, accompanied his daughter to the Haunted House. The *Princess* was pale. *John*, on the contrary, who sat facing his father-in-law in the state coach, smiled with a cheerfulness which in the circumstances seemed a trifle inept, if not underbred. The wedding guests followed in twenty-four chariots. Their cards of invitation said "2 to 4.30 p.m.," and it was now eight o'clock, but they could not tear themselves away from "seeing the last of the poor dear thing," as they agreed to call the *Princess*.

The *King* sat silent during the drive. He was in fact preparing his farewell speech, which he meant to deliver in the porch. But arriving and seeing a crowd about it, and also, to his vast astonishment, a red baize carpet on the perron, and a butler bowing in the doorway with two footmen behind him, he coughed down his exordium and led his daughter into the hall amid showers of rice and confetti. The bridegroom followed, and so did the wedding-guests, since no one opposed them.

The hall and staircase were decorated with palms and pot-plants, and tastefully draped in the national colours of Illyria; and in the great drawing room into which the guests trooped while *John* persuaded the *King* to a seat, they found many rows of morocco-covered chairs, a miniature stage with a drop representing the play-scene in "Hamlet," a row of footlights, a boudoir grand piano, and a man seated at the keyboard whom they recognised as a performer in much demand at suburban dances.

The company had scarcely seated themselves before a strange light began to illuminate that end of the room at which the stage stood, and immediately the curtain rose to the overture of M. Offenbach's *Orphée aux Enfers*, the pianist continuing with great spirit until a round of applause greeted the entrance of the two spectral performers.

Its effect upon them was in the highest degree disconcerting. They set down the coffin, and after a hurried conference in an undertone, the black-moustachioed ghost advanced to the foot-lights, singled out *John* from the audience, and with a terrific scowl demanded to know the reason of this extraordinary gathering.

"Come, come, my dear sir!" answered *John*. "Our contract, if you will study it, does not forbid my inviting whom I choose; it merely stipulates that my bride and I must be present, as you see we are. There is no charge for admission, and the *Lord Chamberlain* and the *Licenser*, would not interfere if they could. Pray go on with your part, and rest assured it is no use trying to ride the high horse with me."

The dark ghost looked at his partner, who shuffled uneasily. "I told you," he said, "we should have trouble with this fellow." They held another muttered conference, at the end of which the leading villain again came forward.

"Our fair but unfortunate victim is suffering from a sore throat to-night," he announced. "The performance is consequently postponed"—and he seated himself sulkily upon the coffin, where the limelight man from the wings promptly bathed him in a flood of the most beautiful rose-colour.

"Oh! this is intolerable!" he exclaimed, starting to his feet.

"It is but so-so, I agree," said *John*. "Still, such as it is, we had better push through with it. Should the company doubt its genuineness"—here he tapped the leg which he had been careful enough to bring with him—"I can go around afterwards and show the brand on the cork."

At this evidence of contract the two ghosts collapsed. They seated themselves on the coffin, and went through the casting of dice, but in a perfunctory and half-hearted manner, notwithstanding the vivacious efforts of the lime-light man.

The tall ghost smote his brow and fled from the stage. There were some cries of "Call him back!" But *John* explained that this was part of the drama, and no encores would be allowed: whereupon the audience fell to hissing the villain, who now sat alone with a most life-like expression of malignity.

"Oh, confound it!" he expostulated after a while, "I am doing this under protest, and you need not make it worse for a fellow. I draw the line at hissing—and confetti" he added, as someone threw a bagful.

But when the ghostly lady walked on, and in the act of falling on her father's body was interrupted by the pianist, who handed up an immense bouquet, the performers held a third hurried colloquy.

"Look here," said the dark-browed villain, stepping

forward to the foot-lights and addressing *John*, "What will you take to call this off?"

"I will take," said *John*, the key which the lady has just handed you. And if the treasure be at all commensurate with the fuss you have been making about it, we'll let bygones be bygones."

Well it amounted to a million of money, rather more than less; and *John*, having counted it out behind the curtain, came forward and asked the pianist to play *God save the King*: after which he bowed his guests to the door, took possession of the Haunted House, and lived in it many years with his bride, in high renown and prosperity.

THE CZARINA'S VIOLET

ONCE upon a time the *German Emperor* wished to be at peace with the *Czar of Russia*. He was at peace already—but he wished to be more so; because he was old, and old men desire to see peace all around them. It makes the settling up of their worldly affairs so much easier; and when they die people say: "*There* went one who saw the folly of quarrelling!"

But unfortunately he was so infirm with age that he could not risk the journey to St. Petersburg. So in his place, with a letter of apology, he sent his *Chancellor*—

who was no other than the famous *Prince Bismarck*.

Prince Bismarck arrived at St. Petersburg late at night. When he reached the Palace, the *Czar* had gone to bed. But the *Lord Chamberlain* was up, and gave him supper, after which he was shown to a magnificent bedroom with a bright fire burning—for Russia is a cold country.

Next morning he awoke to find the sun shining; and being an early riser—to which habit he was wont to attribute much of his success in life—he lost no time in putting on his clothes, to take a walk in the park.

But early as *Prince Bismarck* was, the *Czar's Guards* were earlier. At every corner of the great palace, at the point where every two alleys divided, and at intervals along every well-kept avenue, he found a tall soldier planted. As he passed, each soldier saluted, raising his rifle to the 'present' in five distinct and accurate motions. And this annoyed *Prince Bismarck*, because the birds were singing all the time, and the dew sparkling on the grass, and moreover, he wanted to be alone, to collect his thoughts; for the *Czar* would certainly send for him after breakfast, and there were some nice points to be discussed before the Treaty could be agreed on.

" These *Guards* are a nuisance," said *Prince Bismarck* to himself. " Moreover their uniform clashes in colour with the petunias. There is more wealth than taste in this country."

He walked on and on, until at length it really seemed that he was free of their attentions. For he came to an avenue of pine trees along which no sentries were visible; and at the end it opened upon a level stretch of turf, the like of which he had never seen for smoothness or beauty.

"This is better," he began. But " Oh, confound it ! " he went on, as his eyes fell on yet another soldier who stood stiffly, almost (but not quite) in the centre of the grass plot.

He was moving on impatiently, when it struck him as curious that a soldier should be posted just there. He wanted to be alone, to compose his opening remarks to the *Czar*; yet in all his life he had never been able to pass by anything he did not understand—which was another secret of his success. So he went up to the soldier, who presented arms in five distinct motions accurate as clockwork.

"Excuse me, my man," said *Prince Bismarck*; " but what are you guarding here ? "

"How should *I* know?" said the soldier, who happened to be a Finn, and had not yet learnt Court address.

"But this is curious," said *Bismarck* looking about him, "If you were standing guard by the walk, now—or even in the centre of this piece of turf—though I don't see what purpose that would serve——"

"I stand where I am told to stand," answered the soldier, somewhat angry at being criticized by a stranger.

"And who told you to stand here?"

"Why, the sergeant, to be sure."

This was all *Prince Bismarck* could learn. He walked on. But, as he returned to the palace, there was the soldier still posted, as patient as ever, and guarding nothing at all.

After breakfast he was sent for and held a long conversation with the *Czar*, who, towards the end of it, began to wonder how a man so absent-minded had contrived to make himself a European reputation of the first class.

"I am afraid," said the *Czar* at length, very politely, "I have the misfortune not to make my point clear. If it be a question of how I station my soldiers in Poland——"

" In the middle of grass-plots ! " interrupted *Prince Bismarck*.

The *Czar* stared.

" I—I humbly beg your Imperial Majesty's pardon ! " cried *Prince Bismarck*, recollecting himself and sitting up with a jerk. " The fact is, I saw something this morning which so puzzled me that it has been weighing on my mind ever since."

" Indeed ? " said the *Czar*. " May one ask what that was ?—for we desire to study our guest's comfort in everything."

Bismarck told him.

The *Czar* frowned, for he was considering. " Beyond the pine avenue, you say ? That must be the old archery-ground. . . . Why, yes ! Now I come to think of it, there *is* a guardsman just in that place. I must have passed him hundreds of times : but it never occurred to me to wonder what he was doing there. Let us go and ask him ! " suggested the *Czar* brightly. " We can let the Treaty wait until this afternoon."

They walked out to the archery-ground together. The guard had been relieved ; but there stood a soldier, though a different one, on precisely the same spot ; and he saluted precisely as all the others had saluted.

"Why are you standing here?" demanded the *Czar*.

The soldier trembled a good deal, but confessed that he did not know. The sergeant was sent for, but he knew as little as the soldier. He went in turn to summon his captain, who could only say that every sentinel was posted under the Colonel's directions. This meant sending for the *Colonel of the Guard*.

The *Colonel* explained that in disposing the sentinels he rigidly followed a plan drawn up by his predecessor (an eminent Field Officer, since deceased), and approved by the War Ministry of that day, after consultation with the Ministry of the Interior.

"Do you tell me that you have never shifted a single one, in all this time?" asked the *Czar*.

"May it please you, sire, not one in all these twelve years," answered the *Colonel of the Guard* with evident pride. He mentioned the length of his service, laying a little stress upon it, because the promotion lists had overlooked his name and he had almost began to think his merits forgotten. "Not a single man, sire, by so much as a foot!" said the *Colonel of the Guard*.

"We will look into this after luncheon," said the *Czar* somewhat hastily—for he did not wish *Prince Bismarck* to think his army at any point inefficient. "Meanwhile let a despatch be sent to the *Minister for War*. I wish to be informed *why* this man is standing on this grass plot.

A pretty to-do there was when this message reached the Ministry! The *Minister for War* himself sat for two hours in consultation with all the oldest *Field Marshals* he could summon at short notice: and as for the *Secretaries* and *Clerks* of the department, they tumbled over one another as they hunted through pigeon holes, dived into despatch boxes, dossiers, waste-paper baskets. The dust was terrific; it kept them sneezing all the while.

The *Senior Field Marshal of the Empire* was bed-ridden, besides being very deaf. The *Minister* had to take a cab and call upon him.

"Yes, yes," said the *Senior Field Marshal*, misunderstanding. "The *Emperor* wants to know exactly how I managed to beat the Turks, fifty-five years ago. Well, that is satisfactory, because none of the histories describe it accurately."

As a matter of fact, it was not at all certain that he *had* beaten the Turks. The Turkish histories in particular were quite positive that, on the contrary, he had been beaten. But he began to tell the *Minister* just how it happened, from the very start, tracing out the position of the two armies on the pattern of the bed-quilt.

" But," protested the *Minister*, waving his hands and then talking rapidly on his fingers by the deaf-and-dumb alphabet. " The *Emperor* does not want to know about the Turks. He wants to know why a soldier is on guard in the old archery-ground precisely thirty-seven paces south-west-by-south from the spot where the southern-most target used to stand,"—for these were the bearings shown on the *Colonel of the Guard's* sentry-plan.

" Oh ! " said the *Senior Field Marshal*, not concealing his disappointment. " Well, my memory is not what it used to be ; but I dare say he was put there, to start with, as a punishment."

" But he has been there for years and years and years ! " gesticulated the *Minister*.

" I can quite believe it," said the *Senior Field Marshal*. " Discipline was discipline in my days."

"And moreover, it is not the same soldier! The guard is relieved every four hours."

"To be sure," said the *Senior Field Marshal.* "That introduces a new factor into our calculations. Fours into twenty-four goes eight—no, six . . . six times three hundred and sixty-five, not counting leap years——"

The *Minister* left him to reckon it out and drove back to the War Office in deep dejection of spirits. Towards the close of the day he was obliged to present himself at the Palace and admit, with tears in his eyes, that all his investigations had been in vain. No one in the Army could tell, nor was there any record to show, why the soldier stood on the grass plot.

Meanwhile, and all through the afternoon, a whole corps of *Engineers* had been examining the turf, inch by inch, and they could report no clue.

The *Czar* by this time was so eager to fathom the mystery that he had forgotten all about the Treaty; and so, indeed, had *Prince Bismarck.* Next day it was the same. The *Lord Chamberlain* had sent for all the household and examined them one by one, to no effect. The servants, as they passed and repassed in the corridors, would halt and ask one another: "But how *did* the soldier come on the grass plot?"

On the third day the *Czar* sent around the heralds with a proclamation. He offered the sum of one thousand roubles and a free pardon to anyone who would come forward with the true solution.

In a top attic of the Palace an old woman sat spinning linen for the imperial tablecloths. She was forgotten by everybody save by the little maidservant whose duty it was to bring her meals, and she had bent over the spinning-wheel so long that her body was almost two-double. But in her time she had been nurse to a former *Czarina*—to the present *Czar's* grandmother in fact.

"Dear me!" said the old *Nurse*: "There go the heralds' trumpets, down in the city. *His Imperial Majesty* must be sending out some proclamation or other. I do hope he is not declaring war against anybody?"

"Why, haven't you heard?" said the little maid servant; "It's about the soldier."

"What soldier?"

"The soldier on the grass plot."

"What grass plot?"

"Why the one where they used to shoot with bows and arrows. There's a soldier in the middle of it, standing guard, and every one is wild to know what he is guarding."

"But everyone ought to know *that*," said the old *Nurse*. "Mercy on us, what forgetful heads we do wear in these days!"

"But *nobody* knows!" cried the little maidservant, staring at her; "And the *Czar* is offering a thousand roubles to anyone who can tell him!"

"My child," said the *Nurse*, smiling on her; "that—or a part of it—would make you a very pretty marriage-portion, would it not? Well, you are a good child. Take my arm and lead me downstairs to *His Imperial Majesty*."

So the little maidservant led her downstairs, and when they came into the *Czar's* presence the old *Nurse* dropped a curtsey and said:—

"May it please your *Imperial Majesty*, I can tell you all about the soldier on the grass plot. Years and years ago when the *Czarina*, your *Majesty's* grandmother, was a bride, she held a great contest of archery: for the Court ladies were famous archers in those days,—she being one of the skilfullest. Such a beautiful arm and wrist as she had, too! There is nothing like archery to show off a pretty arm and wrist.

"Well, there the ladies were assembled, one fine spring afternoon, and when they had shot their first flight of arrows at the butts, they were all hurrying forward to count their hits and change ends. But the *Czarina* stopped suddenly, and called on them all to stop. Then she dropped on her knees and they all gathered about her; for there, almost in the middle of the turf, she had happened on the first violet of the year.

"The *Czar*, *Your Imperial Majesty's Grandfather*, came on the ground as they were all kneeling about her in a ring and admiring it. Many declared it to be an omen of luck, for the *Czarina* was beginning to hope for a baby—who in time arrived indeed, and in time became your *Imperial Majesty's* father. The *Czar*, who adored his young wife, at once sent for a Guard and stationed him beside the violet to warn the ladies not to trample upon it as they passed to and from the butts. It was not a very comfortable position for the poor man, there, almost in the line of fire, and the *Czarina*, seeing him wince once or twice as an arrow passed him by rather too closely, called the contest at an end; she had ever a soft heart, even for the humblest. But the *Guard* remained to warn off the common folks; and there, no doubt, he has remained ever since."

"But what about the violet?" asked the *Czar*.

They went and searched. There was not a trace of it. The flower had long since disappeared.

—Yet not for ever. The *Guard* was withdrawn, and in time he in his turn was almost forgotten, and the spot where he had stood. But one day the twenty-second gardener's five-year-old daughter (he had been but the forty-sixth gardener when he married the little maid-servant—so, you see, they were rising rapidly in the world) came running to her mother with a flower she had discovered while playing on the old archery ground.

"See mother! The first violet of the year!"

So the violet had come to life again when the heavy boots of the sentries were no longer there to trample it. But this part of the tale never reached the Palace, where, however, when they have occasion to talk of red tape, they still use a phrase of which few remember the origin: "*But how shall we get the Soldier off the Grass plot?*"

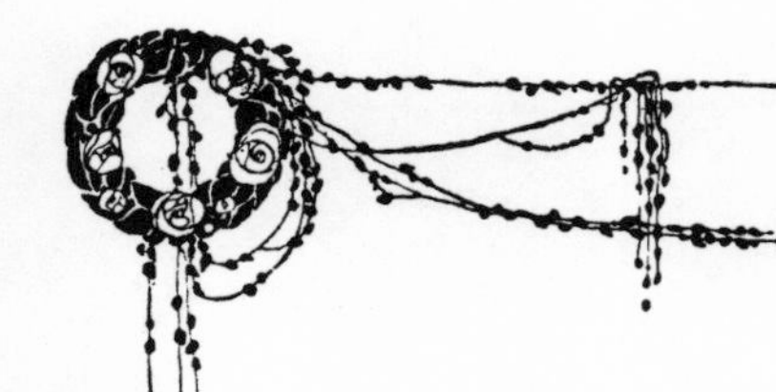

MORAL

Prince! Your armies, horse and foot,
  Cannot kill a violet.
Call your engineers to root it,
Your artillery to shoot it;
  See, the flower defies you yet.
Drum, drum, fife and drum—
Pass and let the children come!